## DESCENT INTO HORROR . . .

I noticed my hand. It was resting along the arm of the chair: perfectly normal.

And then – in front of my eyes it suddenly seemed to . . .

Dissolve.

It flowed into mush. And I could see a mangle of tendons and veins – and heard the blood hiss through them with the sound of a mound of maggots . . .

# The Shadow

**BILL GARNETT**

SPHERE BOOKS LIMITED
30–32 Gray's Inn Road, London WC1X 8JL

First published in Great Britain by
Sphere Books Ltd 1982
Copyright © 1982 by Bill Garnett

This book is a work of fiction and any resemblance to actual
people or institutions is purely coincidental.

Set in 10/11 Compugraphic Times Roman

Printed and bound in Great Britain by
Collins, Glasgow

For Theresa and Jane

'Between the desire
And the spasm
Between the potency
And the existence
Between the essence
And the descent
Falls the Shadow'

T. S. Eliot

# *The Shadow*

# CHAPTER ONE

Drip.

The last drop. It must be. Who could have thought there'd ever be so much?

It falls to the carpet. To the stain. Where it lands, the carpet is still moist and shiny, but the edges of the ring that spread out around that final drop have dried black.

I'm very calm about it all.

I mean, look at me! Could any man be more composed? Note how clearly I'm speaking, how rational and well-chosen my words. Nothing melodramatic about them, nothing . . . deranged.

You are listening, aren't you?

Yes, I believe you are. Your type is hardly expressive, but I believe I see interest in your eyes. Ah, yes – a flicker! Good. It's good to be heard.

It's strange . . . looking around this room, it all seems so normal, doesn't it? The slanting light through the dusty windows. The room itself with its faded furniture. That chestnut tree in the gardens outside, with a scattering of scraggy leaves still left on its branches and, no doubt, below in the street many more leaves that perhaps will be swept into dustcarts before they rot.

A peaceful scene.

Outside, autumn. And here, here in this light high sitting-room, with its nice – if no longer virgin – Wilton carpet, the television is on to the Monday Matinée. On the screen a little girl is skipping in an alley. See how the light from the film plays across Claire's face in her armchair there? Claire? Forgive me – I've forgotten the introductions. I'm Stephen Clements and Claire is my wife.

Where was I?

Oh yes, of course, right here. Where it began. That was . . .

I'm not too sure. Three weeks ago? Two? Imagine not knowing, not knowing something like that! But then, of course, perhaps it never had an actual beginning, but was just a process that had always been going on – like a growth that you carry inside you all your life, but only know about when it suddenly becomes malignant and destroys you.

It could have been like that.

Yet . . .

Of the two alternatives, I rather favour the idea of a beginning and, yes, in that case know when it must have been. That Friday afternoon in October, just after I'd got home from school.

To the telephone call.

It was half-past five. I was just back. It wasn't dark then – they hadn't put back the clocks, you see – and outside the window I could see that chestnut there still massively in leaf. There were kids below it with sticks, throwing them into the branches to try to knock down conkers. They weren't having much luck.

When the telephone rang, I thought it might be Claire, calling to say she'd be late. Her research seemed to be taking more and more of her time then and she'd quite often been late these last months. Instead, though, it was an operator, confirming my number, then saying she had a call for me. There were the series of clicks and wait that you frequently get with long-distance; then a woman's voice with a Cumbrian accent came on the line and, having checked who I was, announced that my father was dying.

How do you react to that sort of news? In my case, as if I'd heard an unpleasant weather forecast. Please don't be shocked when I say that. I know you Orientals have strong family ties, but my father and I could hardly have been less close, and his condition had been labelled terminal for months. God knows quite what he had – some wasting disease the doctors could barely diagnose, let alone treat – but they did know it was doing for him, and so did he. Accordingly, the old man had taken to his own bed, hired a private nurse and was waiting for the end. This was the nurse on the line now, saying my father appeared unlikely to last out the weekend; and that, if I wanted to see him, I ought to come now.

I didn't want to, but said I would.

Claire came in a few minutes later. I told her the news and she said she was sorry and we talked about whether I really had to go – and, of course, there wasn't much question that I did. She suggested I take her Renault, said she'd book me in at 'The George' and call school for me, if she didn't hear from me by Sunday night. She was very supportive and, loath as I was to make the journey, I had enough sense of what the occasion demanded to know there wasn't any avoiding it. I went up and dumped some clothes in a bag and came down and kissed her goodbye.

'Have a good trip,' she said.

Not a very appropriate remark for the occasion, was it? And, you know, as I went out to the car, I had the impression I'd seen a glint in her eyes. Driving off, I thought about it, that look of hers, tried to analyse it. Her expression had been ... furtive – and almost ... eager. Jerking through London's rush-hour traffic in her Renault 4 – that's the one, on the corner there, with the parking tickets on the windscreen – I pondered over what should so excite a long-married woman about her husband's absence. By the time I reached the M1, it had come to me: Claire had a lover. Skinny, moralistic Claire! But then ... why not? Such things may be shocking in your culture, my friend. In ours they're almost the norm. No, you know what surprised me when I thought about that? It was realising that, if indeed my wife did have a lover, I couldn't care less.

Coming from Japan, you might not know that it's as near as damnit 300 miles from London up to Penrith and, even though mostly motorway, in a snail-on-wheels Renault 4, that's a pretty excruciating drive. Almost bad enough to make me wish I'd bought Claire a better car. Still, I consoled myself with how little I'd paid for the thing and how much money I was saving by not taking the train, and gritted my teeth and steered on north into night – with tail and head-lights flashing a meaningless code to my brain and some five hours of road before me in which to think.

I did a lot of that.

Mostly about my father, the man I was driving up to see die. There was a real Samurai, if ever there was one:

dedicated, moral, loveless, as hard as they come. A man of steel, mentally and physically, who you wouldn't believe could be done for by anything less than a tank. It seemed absurd he was going now – a mis-script, like the super-shot of a Western blowing his own foot off – the sort of thing that doesn't happen. Not in any well-directed universe. And, even though he'd been ill for months, I'd never quite been able to suppress the feeling he would emerge to outlive me. Now, slogging north and thinking about the man, I even found my previous acceptance of what the nurse had told me a little surprising. That was what I was feeling, mild surprise – a certain amount of scepticism. Not sorrow, though. Not regret. You mustn't think I felt that.

I've wondered during these final days if this somewhat loveless attitude might have been responsible for what came upon me. . . .

But then, why should it have? There must be thousands of children/parent relationships without love, without even friendship. In father's case, it was hard enough just to think of him as a person. I mean, the man was a caricature: some comic-book fantasy of a soldier that he must have seized upon in adolescence and turned himself into. God knows what most soldiers are like, but surely not like him: absurdly straight-backed, jutting-jawed, his every mannerism an act of aggression, from the way his gun-metal eyes shot down your own, to his handshake – which was more like an act of strangulation. Do you know what really got me about him? There wasn't a day in his life he didn't exercise. I wouldn't be surprised if he didn't make the nurse help him out of bed to do pressups right till the end. Perhaps that was what finally killed him, the exercise.

Jesus, he was actually dying.

Taking with him forever his simplistic solutions and jingoism and disgust at Britain's decline, his DSO from Malaya and whatever memories he may have had of my mother, who was killed by a bottle in a Cyprus riot, when I was a kid. I didn't remember her, but knowing him, believe she was well out of it.

What would he leave me? I wondered without any shame. Precious little compared with what he'd been left. Oh yes –

4

grandfather had been well-heeled. Had made it making hats up there in the north – mass-producing them in the days when they were an essential part of every man's wardrobe – and minting money in the process. Most of which had gone to the colonel, my father.

Hah!

He, as an officer and first-generation gentleman, had shown a proper disregard for commerce, selling the factory and, without ever taking a gamble or doing anything in any way flashy, managing through sober, consistent misinvestment, to lose the bulk of the accruing small fortune. Now he was dying in all he owned: a three-bedroom, rather spooky house in the market town of Penrith – a house which my not very informed calculations as I drove north reckoned as worth perhaps thirty thousand pounds.

Claire would find that sum quite a disappointment.

Dear Claire. Most things about me disappointed her. Not, of course, that she often said so. Not in words, at any rate. Like her ambition, her criticism was seldom overt. She was too clever – and I think at heart confused – for that, but I felt it none the less. The daughter of a city accountant, she said she despised money and I believe that she did – almost as much as she despised men who didn't have it.

I suppose it's not an easy time, this, to be a woman. But . . . you're worried she'll hear us? You needn't be. Not now. Not with the television on, you see.

Ah, my friend, all this might give you the impression I was somewhat out of love with Claire. But, you know, when you're constantly with someone, when you're locked together in a way of life, you cease to think about what you feel for them. I was somewhere on the M6 north of Manchester when I realised that: saw I indeed had only the most minimal affection for my wife – I was surprised at quite how little – and felt a strange relief that this feeling was suddenly out in the open in my mind.

I doubt you'll have been along the M6, but, after Lancaster, the country gets really beautiful, softly wild and hilly to moorlands and mountains and at its highest, just south of Shapfell, the sun sends light and shadow gloriously dancing on the green Pennines. Unfortunately, being night now, as I urged my heap of French tin along the wide road, all I could see was endlessly unrolling black tarmac in the car's inadequate beams.

I could see back with far more clarity . . .

Back over the eight-year span of my marriage. Ah, what a long drive can do! I saw the whole thing: withering attraction, mutual disillusionment, repetitive days and weeks and years – the recipe for a sour union. Held together now by simple inertia. With the flash of a sudden headlight, I thought: perhaps my constant slight feeling of guilt for no particular reason is the result of her conditioning. Maybe it's all those years of her unspoken criticism that's done it, somehow making me feel I'm less than I am. I followed the idea through and it was with my first sublime thoughts of divorce and none at all of death that I pulled at long last off the motorway, went rather too quickly round Penrith's first roundabout, and past the hospital there into the night-time town.

Penrith after dark is no Broadway. In the town centre you will find a lit-up clock, some shops, two banks – and that's it.

I parked outside Graham's the grocers and got out to stretch and breathe. The air was cold and clean and brought a lot back. I'd grown up in Penrith and memories came that night of holidays from school there, doing a Wordsworth and rowing the lakes and walking the fells. I took one more deep breath, then got my bag out, locked the car and went across the road into 'The George'. One's father doesn't die every day, so I was staying at the best hotel. It also, if you don't mind the tweedy company, boasts an adequate restaurant and the town's most congenial bar. I checked in, had a big gin, then went and telephoned. After a while, the nurse answered – jerkily. She'd clearly been asleep and her voice was rough.

Yes, my father was still alive.

No, there'd been no improvement.

No – she was not an oracle – she had no idea of whether or not he'd last the night.

I see.

I paused. You know – one's strange: having come all that way, I couldn't face the final half mile. Not to what was waiting there. So I simply said I'd be round in the morning and hung up and went back to the bar, had two more gins and went up to bed. I was suddenly very tired. I didn't believe that my father was going to die in the night but, if he was, then let him.

So there it is . . .

Call me a callous sod, if you like. But, as it happened, my father didn't croak that night and, after sleeping the sleep of the guiltless, next morning after breakfast I went round.

It was a crisp autumn day. A good day to die, I suppose, if any day ever is. Nice weather, anyhow. No spooky storms or midday hooting owls, or chickens running headless. None of the Shakespearean portents that are supposed to herald a great man's snuffing it. But then, of course, my father was no great man; and like most of us, would come and go through this world without leaving so much as a lousy ripple behind him.

The house was some ten minutes walk from 'The George'. In a clean, evenly proportioned, very English square of quietly prosperous, two-storey, flat-fronted houses. Most of them had been recently repainted and father's was no exception – except that it struck me as just that much better turned out than the other buildings, all shiny-shoed on parade. I stood before the property and upped my valuation of it a little, and at the same time felt a weird nostalgia to be standing once more outside this provincial building that had held, and let go, so many days of my youth.

The nurse opened the door. She might just possibly have been pretty – but a stiff-shouldered uniform like a traffic warden's did for her body, and a defensive and distrusting frown took care of her face. I introduced myself. She eyed me up and down disapprovingly. Then, with every appearance of reluctance, let me in.

I stood for a moment in the dark wood hall. All the old ghastly curios were there: weird Malay death masks and blow pipes and totems, spears and barbed throwing knives and clubs and assorted strange weaponery from all the countries father had ever been stationed – and some that I'm sure he hadn't. Looking at them now, they seemed more than ever sinister and I felt my flesh start to prickle, but I shook that off and went on up the stairs. And nothing was any different there either, except that perhaps the red hair-cord carpet was a fraction more frayed.

The great difference was when I went in the room.

I remember once, when I'd broken my arm and it finally came out of plaster. The thing had wasted to a twig and, seeing it – the shock of suddenly seeing that withered thing where my arm used to be – made me feel sick and faint. It was like that, going into that room.

It shrieked at me. Assaulted me with dark, smell, litter, closeness, the foul reek of death. I had to stand, shut down my senses, then open them – very slowly – and take it all in, piece by piece: no regimental regularity here. A mess of medicines on the bedside table, a cheap hospital water jug. Oxygen bottles near the bed, a bedpan visible beneath it. And, Jesus – the smell! I understand it is not uncommon for advanced spinal cancer cases to give off a putrid odour, but this – this was so nauseous – it was like carrion. Meat rotting in a high sun. The worst, though, was seeing father. His face had caved in and his hair – now quite white – was extraordinarily thin and long and drifting around it like cobwebs. There seemed almost nothing of him left beneath the blankets and the eiderdown above him was crooked. As I entered the room his eyes were shut, but when I turned from closing the door, they had opened and were watching me.

'Straighten up, boy!'

Can you believe that? He didn't actually say it. But it was there, in his eyes – the disapproval – and – the automatic reaction set in: I couldn't help it – I felt myself slouch even more. Whatever had happened, he was my father still.

I came to the bedside. I looked round. The nurse had not accompanied me into the room. I turned back to father and rather awkwardly straightened his eiderdown. He looked at me, made a brusque gesture with his head. At first I didn't understand. He did it again, angrily, and I realised he wanted to be pulled up onto the pillow and I did that. His body was sticks.

There was a chair close to the bed and I drew it closer and sat. I looked at him. There was something else in his eyes now. A grin? I couldn't be sure. But how could he be amused at this moment – and at what? He'd always seemed to me to take everything so seriously. That grin suggested depths in the man I had never imagined and, confused as I already was, it unsettled me more.

'Hello,' I said, to say something.

I tried to smile. I did not call him 'dad'. I'd never wanted or been able to – and often in my mind, I know, I thought of him as 'The Colonel'.

'So . . . you've come to see me die.'

I think he was trying to bluster, but his voice came out a mew. And quite suddenly, with a start of sympathy, perhaps even affection, in a way I'd never spoken to him before, I said:

'You know you can't die, you arrogant sod.'

I almost believed it, you know. He'd always had such a fierce grip on life. Even now it was hard – it was hard – to conceive that the old iron soldier was going.

Then he smiled.

And he had no teeth in his mouth.

I saw they were in a glass on the bedside table. It was another shock because I'd never known that his teeth were anything other than his own, and it brought home the man's mortality and for the first time in my life – too late – I realised that my father, incredibly, was a human being just like everyone else, a man who sweated, peed, hurt, just as others did. And who died as well. I didn't know what to say.

'Brace up!'

He almost managed to bark it. The old look was back in his eyes. I realised that his smile had not been communion, it had been *at* me. Mocking. Me. Slouched in the chair. I stiffened, my sentimentality cold and gone. Consistent to the end, the colonel, oh yes: no time for spineless schoolteachers, be they son or not.

But, of course, he had his duty to do.

'Now, listen: no . . . loose ends.' He smiled. Fiendishly. 'House deeds, money . . . there.' He moved his eyes to the drawer of the bedside table. 'All yours – what there is of it.' And he snorted.

'Thank you.'

He stared at me – with what seemed like a deep sneer –

and I think was about to say something, when a ripple went through his body. I saw it pass, under the sheets, from his legs right up to his face, dazing his eyes with pain. His hand jerked towards me, knocked into the table, upsetting the water glass which contained his teeth and spilling them onto the floor at my feet. My instinct was to bend and recover them – but, before I could move, his hand had found me and his long thin fingers fastened like clamps just above my wrist, so hard that it hurt, and he gave an awful rattling sigh.

God, that was a terrible moment. I was embarrassed, powerless, scared. I wanted to run, had a sudden panic that somehow he was trying to drag me with him. I had to fight to sit on that chair with all that I had. His eyes were closed, his lips fluttering. The hand on my arm was brown with skeleton-wrinkled fingers and extraordinarily long and curved yellow nails. They were digging now, painfully, into my skin and for a moment I had a sense of horror that they were four fiendish tubes that were trying to pierce through my flesh and suck the life out.

God knows how, but I managed to sit there and do nothing, while his grip went tight as a gin-trap on my arm. I did not know what to do, you see, or even where to look. I did not want to watch this man's dissolution, to see death rob him of his final dignity, but every time I turned my eyes from the cobwebbed mess of his face, they'd be drawn to his teeth there on the floor and that was, in its way, worse.

I do not know how long I sat there, not sure if he was even still alive. In the end, the reality of his claws in me was pain beyond what I could stand and suddenly I got this terror that he'd die, and rigor mortis set in, and I wouldn't be able to get his hand off – and they'd have to cut it away, finger by finger, in the morgue. Trying not to be too rough, but really quite scared, I prised it off with my other hand, fought it off – and, my god, he was strong. It was almost as if he was fighting to retain his grip on me like a lifeline. But I wouldn't let him. I couldn't any more. And so I finally unprised his fingers – and it was at that moment that he seemed to let go. He gave a deep rattle and his eyes opened and looked clearly at me with what I believe was hatred. Then they spasmed and closed. I think at that moment he died.

But I stayed there, not knowing for sure. With nothing to say and nothing to think and nothing to feel. Just watching to see if I could detect any breathing. I couldn't and after a bit got up. I opened the bedside drawer. There was a large envelope there with my name on it. I took it and went and called the nurse.

She swept into the room, went to the bed, examined the colonel, confirmed he was dead. Professionally, she said she was sorry. I stood there a moment. I was shaken. I watched her bustle, tidy the bedclothes, even pick up the teeth and glass from the floor. I wondered if she'd pull the sheet over the corpse's face as they do in the movies, but she didn't. Living or dead, its presence was the same to her. She looked round the room then and, finding things to her satisfaction, accompanied me out and down to the hall. I gave her my address, asked her to do whatever one did now, and send me her bill; and then, unable to stay in that place any longer, I burst out and into the street.

God, it was good to get out of there!

The day was crisp and fine and it was almost amazing how normal everything was – the people going about their business their everyday way. A man had died, the world was the lighter by one, but market-town life went on – as it should do – all unaware.

I walked. Appreciating the air and the light, feeling some of the weight of the morning slowly come off a little. Then I found myself outside 'The Crown' and, seeing it was just after twelve, went in for a couple of stiff ones.

I put them down quickly and ordered a third. My god, it wasn't even one o'clock and all that had been and gone. In a space of hours. Right to the end, my father had been punctual: delaying his dying till my arrival, then getting it done in the decentest possible time. A little hysterically, I raised my glass to him. I think my father was more man than I knew.

I drank that third drink and went on to a fourth. I needed it. I could not remember a more harrowing morning. Even my arm was aching from where he had taloned it. I looked at it. Do you know – his nails had pierced through the skin.

There were four . . . four fang marks, just above the wrist. They had bled and the blood was only now drying to scabs. I dipped a finger into my glass and sterilised them with scotch.

Gradually I grew calmer and went over what had to be done in my mind: funeral arrangements, notify his few friends, check through the house that there was nothing I wanted; get a local agent – say David King & Co -- to auction the remaining contents and put the place itself on the market. This was the aftermath of death, sweeping the remnants of a man away. Soon all that would be left of him would be me.

Me.

Rather a joke in its way that, isn't it?

I put the envelope I'd taken from his bedside table on the bar and opened it: last will and testament, house deeds, key, bank statement – £400. Probably just enough to settle what was owed the nurse. He'd judged it fine. I had another drink. Then set about doing what I had to: called the undertaker, managed to fix a fast funeral for Monday; rang those of his friends I could remember who were still alive and asked them to pass on the word. Then it was a question of notifying the auctioneers and estate agents and arranging a time to meet at the house. After which, I'd had enough of that day – and bought a bottle and took it up to my hotel room – and that took care of what was left of it.

Sunday morning came sparkling.

Despite the damage I'd done my bottle, my head was clear. So was my spirit. After breakfast, I decided to visit the house – my house now – and see if there was anything there I wanted. It had to be done and, I confess, I had a sort of curiosity to inspect my inheritance. I suppose it was rather vulture-like, but there it was, and so I went round.

As soon as I'd let myself in, I wished I hadn't.

The dark brown hall with its grim curios was silent, but the presence of the colonel was everywhere. Brooding. An aura so strong I expected at any moment to see him come striding down the stairs and sneer at me, and I had to fight down a desire to call out and announce I was there.

I wasn't a comfortable feeling going through that house.

In fact, it was almost frightening. I could feel the old man walking behind me, his dislike and disapproval stronger than ever – and somehow threatening now he was dead. I went through the place as scrupulously, but as fast, as I could. And it had nothing for me. Even the room I'd had as a child had been redecorated, my memories painted away. About to go, I realised I'd omitted his bedroom. I steeled myself – and went in, but I needn't have worried: the undertaker was earning his crust and the mortal remains of the colonel were gone. Strangely, this one room was presenceless, bare, even the poisonous smell gone. Unlike the rest of the house, this was simply a room now, where he might just as well have never been. I went back down to the hall and stood and looked a last moment at all the ways of death on the walls. I wanted none of it. I left. I was glad to get out and would not be coming back. Let the auctioneers handle it all from here, sell his sinister stuff along with the house. Who knew, maybe the weird-weapon market was up right now.

I got in the Renault and drove away from it all.

I went out to Pooley Bridge, to the Sharrow Bay. That's one of the world's great restaurant, right by the side of Ullswater, with a glorious view and good food and wine – and I did myself well on both. I sat there and looked out across the long, blue, mountain-rimmed lake and it was very lovely and I felt strangely liberated. And not a little unreal. However you looked at it, this beat my normal Sunday routine down at the 'Norland Arms' in Addison Avenue, drinking beer and talking sport and politics and how the world was going to hell.

After a long lunch looking at those mountains, I decided to go out and climb one. So I got in the Renault and drove up round past Howtown to the southern point of the lake, up to where the road peters out into sheep tracks – and there I got out and started to climb.

Being Japanese, I don't suspect you know much about the Lake District, but it's England's only true mountain region and its peaks of volcanic rock thrust up from the floors of hidden valleys to heights of over 3,000 feet. Hah, you say, that's not a patch on Mount Fujiyama. No. But does that have winding lakes that mirror its mountains? Tarns that lie like dark jewels among its crags? Does that have old stone farmhouses, tumbling trout streams, hillsides that blaze at this time of the year with the colour of bracken and heather?

I rather think not.

The particular spot I was climbing is called Place Fell. It's some 2,000 feet high at the top and, when I say climbing – it wasn't really that steep – it wass more a vigorous walk than a climb. All the same, it's exhilarating and for most of the way you see the blue of Ullswater extending in a double curve below you – and that is a good thing to see.

And so you wind your way up – following sheep tracks mostly, and the woollies are grazing there, often perched at extraordinary angles on the mountain side, and there are fell ponies too. As you climb, the heather gives way to thin grass and at the top, rock begins to break through. The summit itself . . . ah, that is a place of almost holy beauty. The air is so sharp and clear. Other mountains roll around you. There is a cairn which climbers have built, and I added a stone. Then I moved down a little to the western side of the fell and gazed out over the lake. From this height it was pure beauty and I sat on the ground and looked at it, away above it – the world, my life – and quite detached from them: a thirty-two-year old schoolteacher, sitting on the heather over a blue mirror in the wind.

Perhaps it was the wine at lunch, perhaps the mountain air, but I felt a – I'm not sure how to describe it – a sense of separateness from myself. I lay back on the ground. It was cold and damp. I didn't care. The wind was blowing on me, you see. More – it was blowing *in* me. Through me, sweeping me on with it, dispersing me over the mountains. Below me then I felt the particles of my body begin to merge with the earth, atom by atom, become a part of it. It's hard to describe that experience of ceasing to be a single entity, of losing one's oneness; but it was good and right, that merging – and in a way it was a sort of dying too. And that was also as it should be.

It was easy to understand then how you – your per-sonality – could be sucked away and you could come down from these mountains, if you came down at all, a shadow –

while the essence of you stayed up there in the wind on the fells.

I did come down. After all, I'm here now, aren't I? Sort of here.

But on the drive back to Penrith, I had the idea I was changed.

# CHAPTER TWO

See the spider there by the stain? This is the second time it has spun its way down from the ceiling to feed. The last time, it so gorged itself, its body became discoloured and so bloated it could hardly move. I did not know that spiders ate that . . .

We buried my father on Monday morning.

I felt strangely unwell, but maybe that's the right way to feel at funerals. I'm not really up on them, but this can't have been much as they go. There was just me and four old codger friends of the colonel and, to lend a little tone to the company, a mongrel dog that appeared from somewhere and stood, looking suitably mournful, while the vicar went through his patter.

I hadn't a dark suit, so I'd bought a black armband for my cord jacket and stood there, watching the dog and old men and thinking they were probably quietly rejoicing that they were still standing – while yet one more of their friends was getting planted. The whole thing had an unreal feel to it, like a play I was watching from miles away and no part of. And, I'm afraid, rather than regretting my father's passing, I spent most of the time wondering how much to ask for the house.

After the ceremony, I met the agent and we discussed it, and he said that any reasonable house in St Andrew's Square should fetch in the region of £35,000 – which was more than I'd thought of asking – and I left him the keys and went away well pleased.

It was lunchtime as I checked out of 'The George' and started the long chug south. I felt better now and, in its bizarre way, this had been a satisfying trip. The old man had had his run. I could not find it in me to regret him. But I was pleased about the money. I couldn't deny that. Pleased too that I'd been given the time and distance to take a closer look at my life.

And now could do something about it.

Possibilities unrolled like the road, but less grey: I'd take a year off, go round the world – and maybe never return. Ah! And why not? I'd drifted to teaching, never had any particular vocation for it, and generally found it about as rewarding as trying to hammer a sponge through concrete. A year away would be fantastic. God knows, I might even discover I had some sort of talent. Who knew what I might grow to, now the weight was lifted – especially without Claire. Claire there, trying to pressure me some way or other that I did not want to go.

I would definitely have to do something about that . . .

Ah, my friend, those were my fantasies then. Almost funny in the light of what followed, aren't they?

A sound, a scent, a glimpse through a closing door . . . it's as well we can't see the future. At least I had a part of that drive feeling free. Whereas – could I have seen what was before me and believed it and, if I'd had the guts – I might have turned my tin trucklet into the opposing traffic and put myself away for good.

As it was, though, I felt . . . invincible. You know the sensation – a certainty that everything, every detail of your day, is going to go just right? One doesn't get it often, but when you do it's like the Hand of Destiny is moving along before you, sweeping every obstacle out of your way.

That's how I felt as, just north of Birmingham, I pulled off the motorway into a service area. It was a typical place of its kind: dirty and impersonalised by constant throughput of people, but as I parked outside the shops and self-service restaurant there, I sensed it had something for me. Something I wanted.

Company. Preferably female.

I looked around the service area. Crumpled families extricating themselves from cars. Nothing there. I got out and went into the restaurant.

Humanity never looks its best in transit, and this place was crammed with some dreary specimens. It was only after I'd shuffled through a food queue, loaded my tray with gunge, and was searching for somewhere to sit that I saw a possibility. She was at a window table alone. A wavy-haired blonde, who looked broke and tarty – and as if she might appreciate a lift to London. I took my tray and zig-zagged through tables towards her.

She was coddling a coffee, staring out through the dark-glassed, lace-curtained windows down towards the rush of the motorway. She didn't notice me as I came up.

'Anyone sitting here?'

She didn't react.

I tried again. 'D'you mind if I sit here?'

When she didn't respond to that either, I sat.

Confidence somewhat shaken, I made a performance of unloading my tray, reaching for ketchup, knocking the salt-shaker on the table. Through it all, she ignored me. I started on eggs, beans and mash, glanced at her above them. Close to, she wasn't exactly a beauty queen, but she certainly had poise, sitting there with a near-empty coffee cup and gazing into space. I forced down my meal, clacked knife and fork together, decided to try yet again.

'You going down to London?'

For a moment, she remained staring out of the window. Then her head turned. I smiled at her. Her face faced me and her eyes looked right towards mine – they were big eyes of an almost frothing green – and they looked right through me. Clean through my head. Dematerialising me before her. I felt the smile turn to rictus on my face.

I averted my eyes, rearranged knife and fork, took one scalding sip of the sewage in my cup – and then just wanted to get out, and did.

So much for my godamned Hand of Destiny!

Angry and unnerved, I paused outside the restaurant and suddenly decided to call Claire. I should have done that days ago. Fine. I found an unvandalised phone booth, poised coins and dialled.

The number rang for some time and I was about to hang up when she answered. Just before the pips drowned it, her hello sounded out of breath.

'Hi,' I announced when my coins cleared the line.

'Oh. It's you.' Still breathless. 'Where are you?'

And then, for no conscious reason I lied. 'Penrith. We planted the old sod this morning, but there's still a lot to wind up.'

'Poor love,' she said, breath back and sounding sincere, 'Is there anything I can do?'

'Call school and tell them I'll be in tomorrow.'

'Right.'

'Thanks. Well . . . I'll see you when I see you.'

'Fine. No rush. Drive carefully now.'

'I will.'

That was cunning, I thought, going back to the car. Now Claire wouldn't expect me back for another five hours. The remaining journey should take half that. Which gave me plenty of time in London to succeed where I'd just now failed . . .

But, as I started the car and headed for the station's petrol pumps, something started nagging in my mind. Claire's breathlessness. She had sounded like . . . how she used to sound when we'd been making love.

I asked for a full tank and thought about that. Was it possible? Could she have a lover in the house? And how long might he stay, with her husband not expected back for five hours?

With my mind on such things, I got my petrol, gave the pump man a twenty. He counted out change, passed it through the window. I held out my hand for it – and the man completely missed it and released the change in mid-air, all over my lap.

Without so much as a 'sorry', he turned away. For a moment I just gawped at his back. Then, mistakenly dismissing the incident as just a new low in the already abominable standard of British service, I put the car in gear and drove off, gathering what money lay within reach as I did. The rest could wait. Right now I had to make miles.

I put my foot down.

Unfortunately, not much happens in a Renault 4 when you do that. After some minutes, I managed to grind the car up to 70 and there was a single downhill high when I actually nudged 80. But mostly 70 mph was it – and, in that car, enough. No solid Jap – sorry, Japanese – motor, the car howled like a tornado and sidewinds would bowl it at other lanes.

It got rather bad, that drive. The road became slick with intermittent rain and, not far past Birmingham, I ran into fog and had to come down to 30. After a little of that, with my face pressed close to the windscreen, my imagination slipped into overdrive. I started seeing ghost shapes flitting across the road; once or twice caught myself braking for things that weren't there; and the fog acquired the quality of tentacles and its long wisps and strands made me think of my father's lank hair. Then I found myself recalling his damned teeth on the carpet and wasn't sure whether I wanted to laugh or be sick.

I must have been tired.

I certainly was by the time I made it to Holland Park Avenue and turned off into Princedale Road towards our flat in St James's Gardens. Flat? Well, it's really a maisonette, but I always say 'flat', because Claire insists on calling it a 'house'. Instinctively, I parked on the corner where I couldn't be seen from the place. And then, feeling suddenly both furtive and strangely excited, all tiredness gone, I left the car and almost slunk down the road to number 31. Quietly, I let myself in.

Our place, as you've seen, is a long streak of not very much, spread over second and third floors, and I went up the communal stairs to our door almost on tiptoe. Very quietly, I got the key in the lock. Did I really want to catch Claire in the act? Yes! Almost soundlessly I opened the door, stepped in. I paused in the stairwell, listening, and did not turn on the light. On the half-landing before me was the kitchen; half a flight up, the sitting and dining-rooms; on the top floor, two bedrooms and a bathroom. You can easily hear to the sitting-room floor from where I waited. I heard nothing.

Which left the bedrooms.

There are thirty-five steps in that place. Most of them creak. I had to transfer my weight very gradually from one to the other and I think it took me five minutes to slink up as far as the sitting-room – and I began to feel ridiculous. And somehow contaminated by what I was doing.

Why be so furtive?

This was *my* place. If anything was going on here, I was the injured party. I ought to behave as such – not somehow connive at my wife's adultery. I started up the stairs. Noisily. And fast. Would I catch them actually at it? What would I say?

I came to the bedroom. The door was shut. I swung it open. There was nobody there.

Not sure if I was relieved or disappointed, I stood a moment. Then, to be sure, went to the other bedroom, which I used as a dressing-room. That too was empty. Feeling thoroughly let down, I shambled down to the drawing-room and flopped in an armchair. I looked round the room. There were no stains in the carpet then, but otherwise it looked just as it does today. And yet . . . it seemed to have undergone some subtle change and I felt almost like a stranger in it and no longer at ease there. Maybe they were at his place. Maybe. But then – perhaps the bitch didn't even have a lover at all. Damn her. That possibility made me feel even more of a fool. I got a glass of milk from the kitchen, went upstairs, took a bath and got into bed.

It felt like five minutes later that I woke. The overhead light was on and Claire unzipping her dress. Glancing over her shoulder, she saw me looking at her.

'Go back to sleep.'

I looked at my watch. Eleven. 'Where have you been?' I demanded.

'I didn't think you'd be back before midnight, so I went to the cinema.'

I wasn't sure I believed her. 'Good film?' I asked snidely.

'Not very.'

She dumped her dress over a chair, peeled off tights and pants together. Her legs were long, if skinny, the skin smooth and thighs still firm . . .

'Damnit!' I exploded, 'I've just buried my father. You might have been here to meet me!'

Hands on her bra strap, she paused, faced me. 'I'm sorry,'

she said. Then turned away, unhooked her bra, leant forward and let it fall off her shoulders. I saw her breasts reflected in the dressing-table mirror. There wasn't much to see.

Shrugging into her nightdress, she sat down at her dressing-table and started brushing her hair. It was good hair. Long, dark and thick – and she cared for it with an unfailing nightly routine: fifty strokes on the left, fifty on the right. Her face always assumed a faraway look as she brushed – and watching her then, I had the notion that I'd like to take a pair of scissors and chop the lot off. Instead, I studied her. Her face had a more than usually dreamy expression: the cheeks slightly flushed, the eyes with a sort of gleam about them. The look of a woman . . . satisfied.

I thought about what that could mean and, you know, rather than anger me, the implications were strangely exciting, and I saw my wife as desirable for the first time in years.

'It was a bloody weekend,' I said.

'Poor love.'

I waited to see if more was coming. It wasn't. The brush now switched to the right hand side. I propped myself up on the pillow and lay there watching – and wanting – her; and even as I did, was aware of the gap that all the years we had shared had driven between us.

She continued her brushing, completed the requisite strokes; surveyed her hair critically, shook it once, smiled slightly; then, all business-like, went to the door and turned off the overhead light. I put on my reading lamp to light her the little way back to bed. She got in briskly, gave me a plastic smile, a quick peck on the cheek and, lying on her side with her back to me, fluffed her pillows, wriggled down into the bed – and settled for the night.

'Night-night,' she said.

'Goodnight.'

I switched off the light – then suddenly thought: I'll be damned if I'll be sloughed off like that, and turned on my side and moved myself against her. I lay there a while with her flesh against me and, as she seemed to be resisting whatever temptations my body ought to evoke, I swung a hand over and cupped her breast. It did not fill my hand. I gave it a squeeze and pressed harder against her – and her body and her breathing and all of her stayed as cool as if there were just some breeze on her back, and not an eager man.

And after a minute or so of this, I wasn't eager anymore.

I turned away from her and settled back to sleep. And to show I didn't care, said goodnight again – but she did not reply, and I got the impression she was already asleep.

# CHAPTER THREE

I woke the next morning feeling strangely dizzy.

The bedroom seemed hazed, like a picture twisted out of focus, its borders uncertain; and, just a little, it moved. I had to squint and rub my eyes before the whole thing settled and, even then, it was some moments before my mind cleared to the point that I knew exactly where I was.

I turned my head on the pillow. Claire wasn't there. That was unusual, I was almost always up first. What was the time? My god, nearly nine! Being Tuesday, I didn't teach first period, started with English Lit A at ten o'clock – but was going to have to move even to make that. And then I remembered that in my antics of the night before, I'd left the car outside the resident's parking zone . . .

I jumped up, started dressing; as I got my shirt on, noticed my wrist. The incisions my father had made as he clawed me, dying, were now four crescent-shaped, puffy marks. An unhealthy blue. Clothes on, I ran down the stairs – and the wrist started throbbing. As I went out to the street and started across the square, I had an ugly moment wondering whether whatever disease had killed him could be transmitted . . .

But that was pushed from my mind by the sight of a traffic warden writing a ticket by the car.

'Have a heart, love!' I panted, coming up to her.

Ignoring me, she kept on writing.

'Come on! I was just about to move it,' I pleaded.

She tore off the ticket. Without even looking at me, placed it in a plastic envelope on the windscreen.

'Officious bitch!' I murmured. But either she didn't hear me, or was inured to that sort of remark, because her gaze as she turned, just swept over me; and she went unperturbed on her way.

I stared at her starched blue back. Bloody police-state lackey. One minute too late – and she didn't even have the civility to reply. In a fit of pique, I snatched the ticket from the windscreen, tore it in shreds and scattered them. A futile gesture, but it made me feel better.

Then I moved the car to the resident's bay outside the house, where I should have left it the night before, and went in and raced through a bath.

Only – in the bath, I noticed my wrist once more. The thing was definitely going septic. I prodded it. It hurt. As I stared at it, ugly fantasies began to squirm in my brain again; but I shook them off, got out of the bath and poured Dettol on the cuts. It stung. Good. I shaved, dressed, and went down to breakfast.

In the days when Claire still tried to keep up with her Hampstead friends, she'd attempted the impossible in our tiny kitchen: the creation of a breakfast 'nook'. The result, crammed in a corner, was a table large enough for two egg-cups, with a sort of bird-pole behind it you perched on. She was sitting there now, immersed in the *Guardian*. I noticed there was nothing laid for me.

I got out a coffee cup, spooned in Nescafe and switched on the kettle. 'Good morning,' I said.

No answer.

'*Morning*!' I repeated and thumped the coffee cup onto the tiny table.

'Morning,' she echoed, looking up at me over her paper, as if I'd just come in. 'What can I get you?'

'I've got it,' I answered; added water to my cup; and sat.

'Oh – right.' And she went back to the paper.

Now, I don't know what you expect from your women in Japan, but something about this cow's attitude was getting my goat. 'Well?' I demanded.

'Well what?'

'You still haven't asked me how it all went.'

'You told me last night.'

'Did I? You've a better memory than I have!'

She didn't reply, had not looked up from her paper throughout our exchange, and rising irritation drove me to say, 'You are my wife, you know. You might at least *pretend* some interest . . .'

Apart from a slight frown, which might have been at something she was reading, she gave no sign that she heard me.

I waited then. Getting increasingly angry, feeling pressure mounting inside me; wanting a row, wanting to tear the bloody newspaper from her hands and even – yes – slap the complacency from her face. But, of course, I didn't do anything of the sort. We Brits are a controlled lot. And, anyway, there wasn't time. I took two sips of my coffee; without a word got up and left.

Her silence followed me all the way out the door.

Slamming it behind me, I ran down the communal stairs, through the hall and out. In the street, I paused a moment, tried to clear a film of rage from my brain. It was extraordinary: mild, gentle man that I am, I'd never felt anything like this before – almost dizzy with anger, heart pounding, body trembling with it. I had to get myself in hand and I stood there outside the front door, consciously trying to relax, making myself breathe. Deeply – in – out. The air was damp with coming rain. It helped. My calmer breathing started to calm me.

Phew!

That sort of tension can give a man heart attacks.

I started walking towards the tube – then realised, if I didn't hurry, I was certain to be late. Hell!

I started to run. I abominate running – as I do most exercise – but I hate being late even more. So I ran. All the way down Princedale Road to Holland Park Avenue. Now, you may say, that's only a few hundred yards. But, in my condition, it was as far as I could manage. I had to walk the rest of the way up Holland Park Avenue to the tube station and my chest was still heaving when I got there.

To find the lift wasn't working.

Feeling the beginnings of a stitch, I started down the stairs – shiny grey steel, sided with lavatory tiles, they curled round grimly forever – and halfway down, I heard a train coming. I had to try for it. Running again, I clattered perilously down the slippery metal, got to the bottom, reached the corridor – ran down it onto my platform. A train was there, doors closing. I jumped at the nearest, managed to get my shoulder to one door, my hands to the other – a standard obstruction technique, so they'd automatically re-open.

Only – this time the doors continued to close.

Irresistably, they pushed my hands back – leaving me pinned, half in and half outside the train.

They kept closing. Tightening. Squeezing me between them, as if my body was simply so much mush to prevent them meeting. And in that terrible moment, I understood that this was total malfunction; that those rubber-faced, automatic doors were going to complete their union; crush me between them. And squeeze my guts and my life out.

I tried to call out for help. As in a nightmare, my breath came out a sigh. Not a single person in that rush-hour train so much as looked at me – at the man whom, impossibly, the fail-safe doors were mashing like a slug in the jaws of a pliers. I could not breathe now. My ribs were egg-shells. I knew in seconds they'd implode – and the blood burst out from my nose and my eyeballs . . .

Then the doors hissed and sprang back.

Released, I lurched inwards; collided with straphangers, fell to my knees; hunkered there, gasping, while blood colours wheeled in my eyes. The train doors closed behind me. The tube moved away, gathered speed – and I looked up into the supercilious eyes of a man regarding me over the top of his newspaper, who then looked away.

Pulling myself up by a rail, I managed to get to my feet.

It was all I could do to stand. The muscles in my legs juddered. I wanted to puke. And, fighting that, I stood there trembling, clinging to the rail. Notting Hill station came. I should have got off and changed there. I did not release my rail. Nor did I at Queensway or Lancaster Gate, and only at Marble Arch could I at last let go and, wedging myself in a crowd of exiting people, push out through those doors.

I was still trembling as I surfaced to drizzling daylight.

There was no question now of making my first class. Nor was there any way I'd be going back on a tube again. I found a telephone box, called school, told them I'd had a slight accident and someone else would have to take my first class. I'd explain when I got in after break, I said – and hung up and went out to Marble Arch and stood in the rain.

I should have been glad to be alive. Should have even seen beauty in the grind of the rain-snarled traffic around me. You are supposed to feel like that, when you've been brushed by death. But I didn't. I hurt. And I was frightened. For the incident had shown me the mouth of the grave, waiting open beneath the simplest of everyday things . . .

Watching the traffic carefully, I crossed to Park Lane, walked down it to a bus stop; after ten minutes, caught a 74b to South Kensington – and from there walked to Queensgate.

I got to school only forty-five minutes late.

From the outside, the place looks like three big, separate Victorian Houses. But, inside, those houses have been knocked into one. The result is long, dark wood corridors. They echoed, empty of children now, as I made my way to the headmistress' office, knocked, and went in.

The office was a shambles of books and papers and knick-knacks. The only thing tidy was the desk. Mrs Greerson sat behind it – a woman in her sixties, with a face like a melting grey candle: her tallow skin, her watery eyes, her every feature, drooping. Almost having trouble believing it myself, I told her what had happened. She listened attentively – she always listened attentively to everyone – and managed to look simultaneously doubtful and sympathetic.

'How very distressing,' she said.

'It was a bit.'

'Do you feel all right now?'

'More or less. A little sore.'

And then I felt I should apologise and did – and she said there was nothing to apologise for, and I left.

I went to the staff room, which was empty, and sat in one of its pre-war armchairs. The chair's sagging springs did not help my bruised back. Why had the tube doors failed? The only answer I could think of was that their automatic sensors had not registered me. But that raised another question. And, though I did not know why, it possessed me with strange unease . . .

The class that followed was not a success.

It was Language, fourth form. A reasonable bunch – insofar as twenty-seven generally rich and over-indulged girls, just arriving at puberty, can be. Actually, they were nice enough kids. But I was . . . preoccupied. Naturally, they sensed it, took advantage – and skived. My fault. Things went better after lunch.

Come the end of the day, I felt almost normal again.

But, out on the street once more, I could not face the tube and queued in the rain for a bus to take me home. Much slower, it had its compensations. Sitting up top and looking over shiny metal islands of cars, stuck like ice-flows in a motionless, rain-slicked Park Lane, was rather lovely in a bleak sort of way.

By the time I got off in Holland Park Avenue, though, I just felt tired. Sore. I went into U.G. Pharmacies, bought stuff for bruises that you put in the bath; thoroughly pooped, carried it home.

'Hi!' Claire called from the kitchen as I came in.

I flogged up the stairs and she came out and met me on the little landing there and actually gave me a kiss.

'Hello, love,' she said with smiling mouth and determinedly pleasant eyes.

I grunted back, wondering why the big friendship; hung up my mac, and trooped up to the drawing-room. She followed.

'Good day?'

'Oh . . .' What could I tell her? And why bother? 'So-so,' I said.

'Poor love. You look exhausted.'

'I am rather. Think I'll go up and have a bath.'

'Can I bring you anything? A nice drink?'

She really was trying. 'Uh – no – no thanks.' And I went on heavily up the stairs, feeling her eyes on my back.

I ran the bath, stripped and inspected myself in the mirror. I had a vertical band of blue-black contusions across my chest. I poured the chemist's stuff in the bath and myself in after it, and lay back in the water. Damn Claire. I thought. She always defeated me by being pleasant. And, when she tried, she could be a lot more. Faintly, I smelt the aroma of veal, my favourite food. And surrendering to the warmth of the bath then, I began to wonder if my ideas of the weekend hadn't been somewhat extreme; if life with her was not really the better way . . .

That's all it took.

Three pleasant words, a bath, the smell of meat at the end of the day – and all my visions of breaking free were hazed. Already, routine was reaching for me, taking me. Soon I'd be incapable of action once again.

Stuck.

And I thought about traps: traps made of gossamer, of wire; made of habit and lust – and all the ways a man traps himself through his life.

I mustn't let that happen to me. Ah, the irony of it! I lay there and thought: I must break out. And now. Because, if I didn't while I still had some impetus left from the weekend, I would never be so primed again.

I made up my mind. I must get a divorce. That very evening, I'd tell her . . .

Hee-hee!

Look – I know you Japanese are sticklers for formality, but Mr Hitachisan is a bit of a mouthful. Do you mind if I call you . . . Hitch?

Of course you don't!

Another thing – you really must stop darting an eye at Claire. Though she's just over there, hunched up by the tele, I promise you she's not listening to a word we say.

So . . .

I marched down the stairs, all full of resolution.

She was in the kitchen, humming over an apple pie. She was pulling out every stop. She'd even had her hair done, I noticed, looked all clean and fresh. And purposeful – which made me suddenly less so. But I sat in the 'nook' and, staring at her back, tried to remember all the things about her I disliked. It didn't help. With her being all wifely over the meal, a blunt 'I want a divorce' would have been like a turd on a prayer mat. I would have to build to this, first start a row . . .

She half smiled at me over her shoulder.

Ah, but Claire could be so charming when she wanted to. I could still feel that after all the years we'd had – and began to feel a shit for wanting to pick a fight when she was being good to me.

She made it no easier. 'I thought it was high time I made an effort and cooked you a really good meal! We've got escalopes and . . .'

'I'm not hungry,' I interrupted.

'Oh,' she said; then went on brightly, 'Well, that's all the more for me then!'

'Yeah. So – what did *you* do today?' There was sarcasm in my question, the implication that whatever she did was a waste of time.

But she did not rise to that either; taking my enquiry at face value, began to answer. The government committee she did research for was looking into race relations for the umpteenth time . . .

I grunted an incendiary comment. She defused it by agreeing.

Almost desperately, I tried to think of some way to aggravate her. But she was being so damned serene . . . and I realised that it takes two to argue, and if she wouldn't oblige me, that was my lot.

'I see you've had your hair done,' I tried, as a last resort.

It wasn't a clever ploy. She was supposed to ask, 'Do you like it?' And I'd answer, 'no'. At which she'd be upset. And retaliate. And in no time, we'd be locked in antagonism.

Instead, she forestalled me by saying, 'Awful, isn't it!'

And, tuned as I was to disagree with her, I heard myself saying, 'Oh, I don't know . . .'

Then she was putting the food on the table and looking me in the eyes straightforwardly, and saying – almost as if she understood part of what had been happening in my mind:

'How about trying to be friends for a change, love?'

I suppose I'm a man of little character. I've rarely been able not to shake a hand held out to me – and I couldn't refuse her offer of friendship then, either.

'Sure,' I muttered and thought – oh well, perhaps tomorrow.

# CHAPTER FOUR

Wednesday. Day of Woden, one-eyed Norse god of war. And, my chest sore and wrist throbbing, I woke feeling I had been in a battle.

Seeing Claire was still asleep, though, I gallantly went through painful contortions to slip out of bed without disturbing her, even tiptoed to the door. From there I looked back. Success. The line of her unvoluptuous mouth was still turned down, the thin lips parted slightly, in sleep.

I went through to the other little bedroom – my dressing-room – and tried to find a clean shirt. But, not surprisingly, Claire hadn't organised any. The only shirt in the drawer was a waisted effort she'd bought me years ago, when she was still sufficiently interested in my appearance to try to improve it. It was a stupid buy – even then – I had too much waist of my own. Now the thing was impossibly tight against my tube-crushed ribcage. Trying not to feel sour, I put on a roll-neck sweater instead, finished dressing – and heard Claire in the little passage outside.

I poked my head round the door and smiled 'Hi!' at her.

And, do you know? Spikey-kneed below a ridiculous baby-doll nightdress, the cow mooned past, ignoring me, into the bathroom and locked the door.

So ... that's what I got for my previous night's irresolution. Not a Japanese characteristic that, but beware of it anyhow, my friend. And, if ever you see it in your soul, you stamp on it hard.

Angry – and mostly at myself – I went down and got breakfast. So Claire felt that one night's effort, one decent meal, fulfilled all her obligations as a wife. Okay. Fine. Our relationship was back on course: two objects moving through the same sphere, but never making contact. Do you know what the mathematical term for that is, Hitch?

It's death.

She didn't come down while I sopped up my cereal, but before going off I made a final attempt – god knows why. I stood at the foot of the stairs and called up, 'I'm off now. Have a good day!' She had to have heard me and I stood and waited, giving her plenty of time to answer. But she didn't, and I left.

Why was I married to this, I thought in a sort of despair as I walked to the bus stop. She'd had a brief, barely explicable, spasm of friendship, then – zap! The wasteland. With not even politeness to stretch across our frozen distance. We shared a dwelling and that was all.

How had it come to this?

It had been lovely in the beginning, you know. I'd written poems about it. Yeah – poems. Okay, so laugh. I suppose it is pretty funny. It's also rather sick.

We met in our first term at Oxford, both reading English, and that's a romantic place with all its blond stone and mists and spires. It has . . . an atmosphere. So many ideas, hopes, dreams have been born there, they live on in the stone – or so it seemed back then. I fell for Claire almost at once. She was never initially interested in me, I'm sure, but with a woman's natural caution never told me so, either, and did come out with me from time to time – I suppose when she had nothing better on. And I? Ah, I was smitten and I persevered and I was the bulldog, gentle and patient, always agreeable, relentlessly tenacious – and in the end I scored. By which I mean we went to bed.

Neither of us knew much about sex at that age. But for a while, what we had was special and we rode the whirlwind; and a year after she got a Second and I a Third, we married – to the disgust of her parents and the disinterest of the colonel – at a registry office in Kensington.

I suppose it was all very adolescent. Whatever we had, marriage soon took care of. I think Claire realised she'd made a mistake almost the first week. I also believe she really tried to make a go of it for some time, but we had so little to build on – and with the deterioration of our sex life, almost nothing.

I suppose Claire thought she could mould me – beneath her left-wing platitudes, she's really quite ambitious – could make me into something, if not successful, at least . . . interesting. But my natural idleness proved too much for her. My decision to teach was a blow, as well. Though, of course, she couldn't openly criticise it, because teaching is socially useful and okay on the left, but – a master of the subtle put-down – she was always able to let me feel her disapproval without ever voicing it. And I lived in the shadow of her unspoken criticism from that day.

What was amazing, really, was that we lasted as long as this. I suppose it just goes to show, my slant-eyed friend, that the strongest urge in the universe is the one to do nothing at all.

Yet on the bus that morning, firmly ignoring an old lady I should have offered my seat to, my memories were nostalgic. Perhaps because it was autumn. My thought of those early days were like slushy clips from shampoo commercials, all intercut with shots of Claire laughing. And, try as I would, I could not recall how the thin-mouthed woman I was married to had come from that Sunsilk girl who used to be.

Such reflections saw out the bus ride and most of the walk to school.

Still absorbed in them, I followed a sixth-former up Queensgate to the door of number 33. The girl pushed it open, went through, held it a moment, looked round over her shoulder and, as I was about to come through, let the door slam in my face. Unprepared, I only just got a hand out in time to stop it breaking my nose.

Now in a private school of 127 mostly well-behaved upper-middle class girls, aged from ten to sixteen, you don't expect that sort of behaviour. For a moment I stopped in my tracks. Then, angry as hell, I pushed on in – I wanted words with that girl. But already she'd scampered across the assembly hall, and now could have been any one of a group whose backs were receding down a corridor. My god, I thought, staring after them, I'd seen some things in my time as a teacher, but this was . . . something else!

The impression grew as the day went on.

I don't know what, but something seemed to have happened to the children in the little time I'd been gone. There was a . . . difference about them, a feeling of distance – as if they were drifting away somewhere I could not reach. An increasing sense of alienation . . .

Why?

Was there some nuttiness in the air? Sunspots, or even an atmospheric aberration that affected their hormonal balance?

I voiced my feelings to the other teachers, as we sat in the staff room, working our way through coffee and essays after lunch, 'Kids seem a bit odd today.'

'Do they?'

'When *don't* they?'

'It's some gig or other.'

'Start of term traumas,' yet another teacher volunteered.

'No. It's a fad,' Miss Newham, our steely assistant-head interrupted, taking control of the conversation, 'A fashion for being constantly different. The time will come when they switch personas as often as today they change outfits.'

That provoked a lively general discussion. Teachers love to talk, and they raised some interesting theories.

None of them touched on horror.

The end of the day saw me back on the bus, on the top deck, staring out through the window.

It was raining hard, as it seemed to most of that week, and in the park by Marble Arch, I noticed a man on a box. I could see him clearly. His clothes were sodden. The rain had plastered his hair down his chalk-pale face. It was running wet. His mouth was open, his features contorted in frantic speech – yet no-one was listening, or anywhere near. He was alone. And I felt the unsettling certainty that, though he was speaking so feverishly, no sound was coming from his mouth . . .

The conductress moved down the aisle, collecting fares.

She took the woman's next to me. I held out mine, said 'Holland Park'. She ignored me. Went on down the aisle. I stared after her a moment, then – no man to kick a gift horse's teeth in – shrugged and pocketed my money. It wasn't often London Transport gave you something for nothing – apart from a crushing on the tube.

Reaching home, I let myself in, called out 'Hi! I'm back' – and immediately wondered why I had.

There was no reply. Perhaps Claire was back, perhaps not. Who really cared? I shrugged out of my mac in the tiny hall outside the kitchen and went on up to the drawing-room.

It was empty but, turning on the tele, I filled it a little with noise. Then I came and slipped off my shoes and slumped back on the sofa here, right here where I'm sitting now; but just as now, Hitch, I took no notice of the box. You see, I had this sensation. Was it premonition? Did this flat containing so much of Claire just depress me? Whatever, I began to feel increasingly . . . uneasy. Found I was unable to think in a line, my mind flopping from one thing to another, like a landed fish desperate for the water. And everything I thought about was grim.

Perhaps because of my arm.

It was throbbing and swollen and hurt. Though in better shape, I reflected, than the hand that had infected it. By now that hand was probably putrid. So much garbage. My mind constructed a jagged montage: my wrist – his hand – coffin – dust . . . I wondered how long a corpse takes to decompose.

Then I heard Claire's key in the lock.

'Hi!' I called, glad for any company then; and I got up and went out to the drawing-room landing.

Down by the kitchen, she took off her coat before looking up and saying, 'Oh, it's you.'

'Of course it's me. Who did you expect – Robert Redford?'

She came up the stairs, peered at me curiously. 'What're you doing there in the passage? You look . . . guilty.'

'Jesus! I came to say hello.'

She walked past me, poked her head round the drawing-room door, saw the television on. 'Ah!' she said, 'I see.' And she turned and went past me up the stairs.

'Anything wrong with watching television?' I called at her back.

'Nothing at all.'

Like hell. I knew her views on tele. She held it in purest

contempt – along with those who watched it.

'I was only watching till you got back,' I said defensively, following her up.

'You can watch all night, as far as I'm concerned,' she threw back after me, and went into the bathroom, closing the door.

'You wouldn't notice if I did or didn't,' I told the door.

No reply.

Angrily, I continued, '*You're* not always the world's most stimulating company, you know.'

She didn't answer that either, and I tried the doorknob; but found it locked.

'Half the time you carry on as though I'm not even there!' I shouted; and, when there was still no answer, stomped downstairs, turned the television's volume to maximum – and hoped it would blast the bitch off the bog seat.

Of course my behaviour was childish, my eardrums the only loser. Quite quickly I capitulated, turned the set down, then off. I felt at a loss. I wanted to tear through the membrane of indifference between us; wanted Claire to notice me, respect me, damn well react when I entered a room. Or so I reasoned then.

But perhaps a psychiatrist would have said what I really wanted was to hurt her.

She came down after a while.

By then I had settled on the sofa with the morning's paper. She came in, said nothing, sat in an armchair at the other side of the room and started on some paperwork. And so, like so many times before, we went into separate evenings – in the same room, worlds apart. I watched her over my paper, her thin mouth hard and straight as she concentrated. An idea began to form in my mind . . .

And I felt a warm sticky fluid run down my arm.

My septic wrist. The puncture marks had opened. Blobs of brown ooze were worming from them down my forearm. I stared at them, revolted. They had an almost serpentine motion, a foul rotting smell. Getting up quickly, I went to the bathroom, put my wrist under the tap. When I'd washed away the initial slime, I made myself squeeze out what pus remained. There was a lot. When it was finally gone, I dried and disinfected the marks.

Strangely then, in front of my eyes, I saw the inflammation go down, the livid colour subside. Already the throbbing had stopped. The marks looked tiny. Harmless. Next day, they would be gone. Like my father.

Gone to the land of the dead.

Where I soon would follow.

# CHAPTER FIVE

The following day I went back to the tube. I can't say I wasn't apprehensive. I was. But I reasoned that if I didn't take the damned thing now, I'd never have the nerve to again.

I was very careful of the doors. They gave me no problems. Unlike the passengers, who that morning seemed even more pushy and savage than usual. One man stamped on my foot; another kicked my kneecap, when I finally got a seat; neither apologised. A sad reflection on our society, you think? Maybe. But who are you to talk? I've read that in the Tokyo subway you have special 'buttocks shovers' – *shiri-oshi*, I think you call them – just to cram more passengers into each train; and that sometimes they do their job so well, people get crushed to death!

Mind you, I'm sure you make better doors.

Certainly than the entrance at school. When I got there and tried pushing open that door, it was so heavy and sticky, it felt like I was trying to force it open underwater. One of the little dears must have found a way to sabotage it. Jesus, the place was getting more like St Trinian's every day, I thought only half humorously, and any time now, I'd have to watch out for buckets of water over the classroom doors!

There weren't any buckets. But what confronted me that morning was, in a way, far worse.

My first class was English Literature 5. I got there at precisely 9:10, shut the door, went to my desk, said 'Good morning!', as I always did.

But this time I don't believe that one of the twenty-five children in that classroom replied.

I'd never had that happen before, and for a moment just stared at them. Such a unified lack of response took organisation, I realised. It would need careful handling. So I simply looked at them, said 'all right', told them to turn to the appropriate page in their text books – and got on with the lesson.

It was not a success.

They whispered among themselves; twitched and fidgetted; looked vacant when I addressed them. Half the time, they were clearly not listening – and, when they did ask questions, seemed to do so just to play me up.

Now this school was no blackboard jungle, and as one of only two male teachers in the place, I'd never had trouble making my mark before. Today though, my personality seemed totally ineffectual – and it was a double shock: an affront to my teaching and also, somehow, my masculinity. I'm afraid I over-reacted: found myself hammering my desk, once or twice shouting; and ended the lesson by handing out lines.

It was a strangely unnerving experience. And the classes that followed were, if anything, worse.

The best was Sixth Form Literature. The kids here were the oldest in school, taking A levels, and mostly taking them seriously. Yet even their behaviour, the way they looked at me, was . . . odd; and, as if seized by collective deafness, though I was speaking at my normal pitch, they kept saying, 'I'm sorry, sir, I can't hear you.' So that, by the end of the lesson, I was hoarse from constantly having to raise my voice.

Only one girl there seemed unchanged. Linda Durnell. Unlike the other sixteen-year-olds, whose lives still revolved mostly round ponies and country weekends, it was hard even to think of her as a girl. She was so clearly a woman. A long-legged, full-breasted, honey-blonde wet dream – and, god knows why, for the last few months she had fancied me.

She had made that increasingly clear. I can't say I wasn't tempted, either.

Christ, if Linda was a virgin, I was a monk. And her body was one of the most luscious I'd ever seen. But so far, I'd managed to hold off . . . I liked to think, out of principle; but in reality, because I did not want to lose my job.

Today though . . .

Last to leave class, she approached me, her bra-less breasts so ripe beneath her T-shirt, they looked about to burst. I swear her eyes smouldered. I could feel the pull of her body from four feet away. She was worried about her Shakespeare paper, she said. Could I spare half an hour after school to give her some coaching? Just half an hour. We could go to her place round the corner. Her parents were away. She wished I would . . .

I can tell you I wanted to. As much to get back at this bloody day as to have her. But, for some damned reason, I said 'no'.

She came a step closer, looked me in the eyes. She knew I wanted her. 'Later in the week, then?' she smiled.

I took a step back. I had to. Otherwise, I'm not sure I could have prevented myself from reaching for her there and then in the classroom. 'All right,' I nodded. And, while I still could, I turned and left.

In my last class, there were no such temptations.

It was Remove, the youngest batch, between ten and eleven years old; and, though sophisticated beyond their years, still generally sweet children. And yet – they behaved so untypically, so strangely, that come 4:30 and the end of that final lesson, I felt there had been a change in the very nature of things – that, more than just sharing some phase, almost everyone I taught was going slightly insane . . .

Of course, being an educated Englishman and not one of you jibbering Japanese, I quickly rejected that idea; told myself it was simply one of those days; and, sitting at my desk as the children tumbled out, started packing essays into my briefcase.

'Please, sir?'

I looked up to see Marion Little, a dark-haired, serious child with pixie features. Ten years old. And I suppose it says something for my personal magnetism that – not counting the lascivious Linda – she was the only girl in the entire school who, as far as I knew, had any sort of crush on me.

'Yes Marion?' Tired though I was, I had such a sense of alienation from the kids, it was good to be actually talking to one.

She stared at me. Huge-eyed. Obviously with a major case of the miseries, for as I looked back into her earnest little face, I saw her eyes start to brim with tears. She stared at me like that, quite unselfconsciously.

Then she said, 'Don't, sir.'

'Don't what, Marion?'

'Don't go away, sir. *Please.*'

I couldn't help smiling. 'I'm not, Marion. Not going anywhere.'

'Really?' She looked at me with the half-hoping, half-distrustful, expression of children who want to believe – but suspect another adult fob-off.

'Of course!'

'You . . . *promise?*'

'Yes, I promise. I'm not going anywhere. Well – not for some time, anyhow.'

She stared piercingly into my eyes. But whatever she saw there did not reassure her. Her lips started to quiver and she shook her head, and turned and ran out.

Jesus, I thought, as I packed up the remaining essays and left, the poor kid was mental. She should see a psychiatrist. Or so I tried to tell myself. But her strange behaviour touched me with unease. And an inexplicable sense of foreboding.

Walking back from the tube, that sense was still with me and I called in at Rackham's off-licence for some beer.

I needed a drink. I felt unusually . . . weak. My clothes seemed to have added weight and it was as much as I could do to carry my briefcase of essays. After standing some while in the shop, while the licensee there stacked bottles and blithely ignored me, I thumped the case down on the counter. That jolted him into service. I bought a six-pack of Fosters. Ten yards out of the off-licence, their weight felt like so many cans of lead in my arm.

I lugged myself on; passed the Islamic Association in Penzance Place, where a group of Arabs were making throat-clearing sounds at each other. Two houses from mine in St James' Gardens, I saw a black blob on the pavement.

A dead cat. It lay on its side, mouth drawn back in a grimace over spiky teeth. Whatever had killed it had squashed it nearly flat, and its single upturned gelatinous eye bulged horribly from a bloodcaked head. God knows how it had got there. It looked like it had been dead for days. It was a black cat and – though I'm not superstitious – there was something so frankly disgusting about the thing that I stepped off the pavement, and walked around, rather than past, it.

Still half looking at it, I went up the steps and let myself into my building. As I shut the door, though, I glimpsed something else. Something out in the gardens. I only had a flash of it as the hall door closed and at first didn't register what I had seen. It was only when I reached the flat and was dumping briefcase and beer in the kitchen, that I realised. The impossible, horrible thing.

I had seen a human head growing out from the trunk of a tree.

A large brown head. Protruding bodiless, neckless, some four feet up, from the gnarled brown bark of a chestnut. The vision flashed to my mind with appalling clarity. The head had been shaggy. I had the impression of a gaping-mouthed face. It was impossible, crazy. But I realised beyond doubt what I'd seen, and my skin went cold.

Slowly, I went up the stairs to the drawing-room and, simultaneously compelled and strangely reluctant to, stepped to the sash windows overlooking the gardens. I made myself look out. There were lumps on several trees. But all were growths of bark, and none of them now like bone and flesh.

I turned from the window. At once relieved; then worried. Because anyone who imagines heads in treetrunks is starting to shuffle towards the funny farm.

Trying to push the thing from my mind, I went down to the kitchen; ripped off and opened a can from my six-pack, and raced it down. I wanted to talk to someone. Anyone. To tell them about this weird day. Even Claire would have done. But tonight she met for dinner with her co-researchers – or so she said – and wouldn't be back till much later. Come to think of it, she'd probably scoff herself stupid at my story, anyway. Most people would.

I took another can of Fosters and the briefcase and went back up to the drawing-room. I looked once more out of the window. The gardens were just gardens. I turned away and, settling back on the sofa, started marking essays.

The subject I'd set was a hoary old favourite – 'A Ghost Story' – and, as usual, the kids had attacked it with gusto. There were stories of how they dressed up in sheets and scared their friends; there were vampires, werewolves, ghouls, headless monsters, and some charming drawings. Typical eleven-year-old stuff.

Except one.

It was titled *The Membrane* and, unusually, its hero was a man. A scientist who invented a transparent substance that was both unbreakable and elastic. But the substance becomes alive and envelopes him. It then contracts. He screams unheard, claws out against what he cannot see – and is simultaneously suffocated and crushed to death.

The substance then engorges him.

Putting the essay down, I found I felt shaken. The thing had been horribly effective – and I could not believe that either the writing or the idea were that of a child.

So I looked for the name at the top. There was one girl who invariably copied essays, if she could find them on the right subject. This, though was Eileen Patterson.

And that was strange.

For, though I thought I knew the names of all the girls in my classes, I could not recall or put a face to this one.

I got up, went to the kitchen and started cooking. It was aggravating not to recognise the child – more than that, it was bloody stupid. I would check her out first thing tomorrow, but that didn't stop me from being angry with myself now. And the anger persisted throughout my meal and the remaining essays – to which I applied a lot of red pencil.

When I'd finished the marking, I still felt dissatisfied. I turned on the tele. The choice was football, murder, how to grow turnips, or someone telling me about God. I went up to bed.

I took off my clothes in my dressing-room, put on pyjamas, went through to the bedroom, sat on the edge of the double bed that more or less filled it. Critically I examined the room. It did not fit with my picture of Claire. Far too feminine and fussy. Pink walls. Pink lace frills on the bow-shaped dressing-table, little figurine lamps on top of that. Precisely the sort of slushy decor I hated.

When I was free, I fantasised, I would wall my bedroom in black leather, and suspend my bed from the ceiling on chains.

I flopped into bed and switched off the light.

I closed my eyes.

'Stephen!'

Someone was calling me.

'Ste . . . phen . . .'

The voice came from distance. Echoing. With a sense of space around it. It was a woman's voice, softly insistent; compelling me to . . . to answer. To wake.

I opened my eyes and looked into blackness.

I lifted my head from the pillow, staring out, wondering, still heavy with sleep. I could not hear the voice anymore, but slowly my eyes began to adjust, and I could make out things in the room.

It was not the room I had gone to sleep in.

It was larger than the pink room, much larger. I could not see the bedside wall to my left, which should have been only feet from my face; and far down at the end of the bed, past where the frilly dressing-table should have been, a huge mirror glistened darkly.

Not understanding and afraid, I felt my eyes drawn into the mirror. There was depth there. I could not see myself or the bed reflected, but gradually my eyes made out what looked like . . . a dusty store. It was piled with objects and they were so intertangled that it was hard to make them out individually: books, chairs, boxes, lamps, stuffed animals, pans, old gramophones – objects heaped upon objects to the point where they lost their natural form.

And all of them were covered with dust.

Increasingly afraid, I groped for my bedside table and the lamp there, but my hand found no lamp switch, no table. I reached down to the floor to work up from there – and I could not feel the floor. Near panic, my eyes swung back to the mirror. I could see more now, deeper. Between the piled objects was a space, and through it a corridor stretched back into darkness.

Someone – something – was coming down that corridor.

I tried to scream, to rise, to run – but my throat was stopped, my muscles frozen. The thing was nearer. Almost on the borders of my vision. I screwed shut my eyes, with all the force of my will heaved out against the room, the corridor, against everything that contained me . . .

And was thrashing on the floor in light.

In the pink bedroom.

I was on the carpet, by my side of the bed, had pulled the lamp off the bedside table there, and its cord was tangled round my hand. Claire was sitting up in bed, her light on, looking down at me sleepily, annoyed.

'What the hell are you doing?'

For a moment I gawped at her. Then, feeble with relief, I stumbled up to kneel on the bed and, with the instincts of a child, tried to reach across it and cuddle against her.

With an angry 'For Christ's sake!' she pushed me away.

I suppose more than anything that brought me back. I backed off, got up, picked up the bedside lamp and replaced it; and, mumbling an apology for waking her, I explained I'd had a terrible nightmare.

'That's what you get for drinking too much!' she snapped and lay back and turned off her light.

Back in the dark, I was instantly afraid again. I reached for my lamp, found the switch, worked it – but nothing happened.

'Do you mind if we keep the light on?' I asked.

'Yes. I do. Go back to sleep, for heaven's sake!'

But there was no way I could do that. Not in that room in the dark. So I felt my way to the bedroom door and out into the passage. There, I put the light on and that was instantly better. I went down to the drawing-room then and sat in front of the electric fire, with all the lights in the room on – and shivered and at the same time was aware my pyjamas were drenched in sweat.

It could only have been a dream, of course, a nightmare. And yet – it had seemed appallingly real. I shuddered. I would not think about it. But I would not go back to the bedroom and the darkness, either. I went to the kitchen, made myself a cup of hot chocolate, came back to the drawing-room, and settled on the sofa.

Eventually, I slept there. I did not turn out the lights and my sleep was shallow. I dared not sleep deeply, you see. Because all my instincts told me that, if I did, I might be somehow drawn back to that dusty room.

And this time not return.

# CHAPTER SIX

Friday.

Bad Friday.

And a sensation of pins and needles as if a tattooist had run amok on my body throughout the night – with some implement that was drugged. As I opened my eyes and sat up on the sofa, the room lurched; and I had to lie back – in the grip of a sudden nausea so strong it had me sweating.

Closing my eyes, I tried to find something solid inside myself to hold onto. What had I done to deserve this? A horrible dream, a night on the sofa, seemed in no way enough; and, as well as feeling sick, I was worried.

I heard the floorboards by the door creak. Claire had come in. I could sense her standing and staring at me. Knowing what the look on her face would be, I did not open my eyes.

'If you don't get up now, you're going to be late for school,' she told me.

'I . . . don't think I'm going to be able to make it.'

'Not again!'

'I feel . . . awful.'

'The amount you drink, I'm not surprised!'

That's unfair, my mind protested; but too weak to argue, I simply said, 'Look – can you do me a favour? Call and tell them I've got 'flu or something.'

'Why should I do your dirty work for you? I'm not your secretary, you know!'

*Please* . . .

She snorted. But said nothing more, and after another moment I heard her leave the room. I suppose she telephoned, but I never knew; because I fell almost at once into a bilious sleep and, when I woke an hour later, she was gone.

I felt better. But not much, and holding to the bannisters, went weakly upstairs to the bathroom. There I discovered just how weak I was. It was all I could do to unscrew a bottle of Alka-Seltzers; and the glass of water I then took them in had the weight of stone, rather than liquid, in my hand.

I made it to the bedroom and crawled into bed and soon slept again. But my sleep this time was strained, the bed-clothes constricting as a straightjacket around me – and feebly I pushed against them, sweating, as I dozed.

All the same, when I woke at lunchtime, my inexplicable fever – or whatever I'd had – was gone.

I rose, dressed, went down to the kitchen. I was hungry – and strangely restless – and, after wrestling with a super-blunt can opener, mined my way through to some stew. I spooned it down cold from the can. I was suddenly keen – no, damn near desperate – to get out of there. And half way through the brown mush I was eating, I just put it down and left.

Outside, the day was clear, very fresh – one of those rare, pre-winter London afternoons so clean they almost hurt. The garden keeper had a bonfire going in the square's gardens and its smell evoked gone years. I took in great lungfuls of air as I went along the street, and for a while felt free and good and full of sweet nostalgia for – god knows. Because by the time I had sauntered round Saint James's Gardens, admired its chestnut trees heavy with conkers, and strolled down Addison Avenue to the main road, that nostalgia had turned into formless apprehension.

I stood on Holland Park Avenue and watched the mindless traffic stream past up the road. And I thought – I have been sick. Perhaps still am. And something – something in my world – has changed, is changing, and I don't understand what, or why. And do you know, Hitch, standing there alone by the side of the streaming traffic, I almost felt I wanted to cry.

Pathetic isn't it?

But then, we can't all be Kamikazi pilots – and each to his own kind of guts.

Ha!

Peep-peep. Screetch. Bleep. Squeak. All that traffic was hopping and popping by, noses in tails, all tin . . . running and humming along. And I was a bubble apart. I thought of that essay – *The Membrane* – and I felt I was in it there by this metal flood, and I wanted to reach through it and into those cars to the people inside. But bubbles just burst on tin, burst on their bonnets and are wiped by their wipers away.

I stood by the road, feeling lousy and alone.

Then I started walking; scrutinising the faces of the people I passed; stupidly half-hoping I'd meet someone I knew. But of course I saw only foreigners – Yanks from the Kensington Hilton, and fellow countrymen of yours with their inevitable cameras, and other riff-raff of London, where there are so few Englishmen left. The street was just strangers. More bubbles. My god, the loneliness of a city – where does it all come from? I knew where it was going. Into me. I turned and walked briskly home.

Back in Saint James's Gardens, school was out. There was the usual mob of kids beneath the chestnuts, throwing up sticks to try to knock down their conkers and, as I passed, one of those sticks fell back and nearly brained me.

'Watch it!' I yelled.

And those idiot children just gawped at me – as if I'd at that moment materialised from the pavement!

To my surprise, Claire was home when I got there; and, even more surprising , for a moment I was almost glad to see her. I went into the kitchen where she was finally attacking about a week's washing up.

'Hi,' I said.

She went on with the dishes and did not reply. I squeezed myself into the wretched 'nook' and sat there and watched her back.

After a while she turned, saw me, said 'Oh, there you are.' Then added acidly, 'Feeling better are you?'

'A bit.'

'Good. Then you can give me a hand. In case you've forgotten – we're having the Walshes and Jamesons to dinner!'

Like the way I do that Claire imitation? Not bad, is it? Mind you, she sounded much worse, bless her – really scratchy – just like chalk on a blackboard. And Jesus – the Jamesons and Walshes! Of all her left-wing Hampstead trendies, they took the cake. A diplomat and a man from the

Beeb, their wives like two smiling scalpels – all of them so frightfully clued in. Who could ever forget they were coming to dinner?

'I want a divorce,' I said.

I said it! For a moment I was astonished. The words had come out all by themselves, unintended; but their release was a wonderful moment. Only that, I'm afraid, a moment. Because Claire just went on with the dishes as if she'd never heard.

It was purest anti-climax. Infuriated, but controlling it, I said through my teeth, 'I said – I want a divorce, Claire.'

She turned from the sink. In a perfectly natural way, handed me a plate to dry. And, looking for some reaction that never came, from force of habit I took the plate and began to dry it.

'*Well*?' I demanded.

'Well what?'

'You heard me!'

She passed me another plate with a cheerful 'You really must speak up, you know. I can't hear a word you're saying.'

That did for me.

I didn't know if she really hadn't heard or, with incredible deviousness, was simply outmanoeuvring me – but as suddenly as it came, my resolution crumbled. I couldn't bring myself to go through it all again. I went on drying up.

After a while, that grew to be quite a strain. The plates became leaden, my arms ached. Somehow or other, my strength seemed massively sapped, and drying dishes about as much as I could do. It was absurd.

Finished at last, I went to the drawing-room and looked out of the window. Gold in the chestnuts, silver in the birch, a few fallen leaves on the muddied grass. And rain now. Much as it is today, Hitch, much as today. Only, looking out into the gardens then, I could feel myself start to drift out to them, to flow away and out to them – as if there would soon not be any more me.

It was like the feeling I'd had up north on the fells – only this time it was frightening. And I felt it for the ebbing of death.

I looked away from the window and around the room for

some sort of anchor, but all I saw made me quietly desperate; and I knew I had to get out from whatever syndrome this was, and didn't know how to – and suddenly all I wanted was to crawl back into bed.

I went and told Claire I was poorly again. She looked at me like she thought I'd always been that and said, 'You *will* make an effort this evening, won't you?'

Sure I would.

What a party that was!

Let me give you the cast: carefree Claire and I, you already know. Which leaves the Walshes and Jamesons. All of them contemporaries of ours at Oxford and, with the exception of myself, as closely linked as lies in a manifesto.

Roger Walsh was a little blond bomb of a man. In the Foreign Office, a career civil servant – vigorous, self-assertive, blunt, bright – he thought it great fun to play tennis at Christmas and, I'm sure, jogged a grinning two miles each night after work.

Martin Jameson was the man from the Beeb, with a Sunday news programme and also a column on the F T. He had a smooth, discreetly self-satisfied face. And his large house, nanny, two cars and huge income did not seem to him in any way to conflict with his loudly-asserted views about distribution of wealth.

As for the wives – Sandra and Lucinda – they seemed to me interchangable. Except that Sandra had better legs. Otherwise, both were long-haired brunettes, with attitudes and mannerisms formed years ago at Oxford, and who'd remained fixed ever since as pampered undergraduettes. They were people of two modes – either flirtatious or intense – which may be charming in a young girl, but I found downright harridan in women pushing middle age.

So these were the guests. And, oh yes, I believe they had one other thing in common – a mutual contempt for the appallingly unmotivated, politically uncommitted, school teacher, whom poor Claire had the misfortune to marry – but had stuck loyally by.

The slobs.

And yet ... I envy them, my friend. For they are wherever they are. But I am here.

52

Anyway, I spent the afternoon in bed. At six o'clock, some two hours before her guests were due, Claire came up and started going to work on herself. First, the long spell in the bathroom. Then, in dressing-gown, in front of the mirror, on the face.

It was a performance I'd once found intriguing, but which struck me now as a little sick. I watched her peering intently at herself and wanted to say, 'Why bother?'. The lines were there. Soured round the mouth, frowned into the forehead. The powder and creams would not hide them – at least not from the hawk eyes of those Hampstead Harriettes. Behind ingenuous smiles, they would be pecking her face apart. And finding it no competition in the preservation stakes.

An ocean removed from this woman, two eyes on a pillow, I watched her; wishing without passion I could be somewhere, someone, else.

For one of the few times that week, she suddenly addressed me without being spoken to first. Tilting her head to look at me in the mirror, without turning, she said:

'Do try not to get too drunk tonight, will you.'

'Why?'

'Don't be inane!'

'So who notices, anyway?'

Lips compressed, she turned her eyes back to the mirror and went on with her face-work. She'd had her say. Our conversation was done.

I got out of bed – but something was definitely off – decided malfunction: head balloon light, but the razor heavy when shaving and later, putting on once-trendy corduroy suit, the trousers garotted my gut and the jacket hung like a hump on my back. Maybe I ought to diet – or drug – I thought ineffectually and went downstairs, leaving Claire at the hairspray stage in front of the mirror.

In the drawing-room I checked the time and that the place looked okay. And, so freaky is human nature, I was now almost looking forward to this evening. Masochism? Loneliness? Whatever, I went around the room, trying to make everything a little better: moving a chair to hide the cigarette burn in the carpet, puffing up our worn cushions – and for a moment I saw it all through Claire's eyes and

felt a fleeting sympathy for her. It wasn't much – not compared to what her friends had – poor cow.

But my sympathy did not last.

If Claire did not like it, why not admit it; throw off her
half-baked notions of loyalty; and get the hell out? Maybe I'd
feel less sick then. Stronger, I thought absurdly – as I tried to
draw the curtains, and they barely budged. I gave them
another try. Nothing. And then I imagined pulling too hard
– and the huge damned things coming down and burying me
beneath them, just as the guests trooped in . . .

What a joke, I thought – and then no longer found it
funny. The vision changed. I saw myself lying trapped
beneath the heavy fabric, for some reason too weak to crawl
out from under it. I saw myself lying there, slowly suffocating to the sound of their laughter around me in the room.

I let go the curtains and went and sat down.

Claire came in some time later, immediately spotted the
half-drawn curtains and flicked them closed. She turned and
gave me a business-like smile. Perhaps having people to
dinner reminded her she was my wife. I noticed she was
wearing an old black dress, one far less fashionable than
some of her newer clothes. A deliberate ploy, I suspected. To
show how her husband couldn't buy her anything better –
yet how good she managed to look, despite his inadequacy.
Oh, yes. That dress put the evening right back in perspec-
tive, my slant-eyed friend, and I no longer looked forward to
it at all.

The bell rang.

They all jazzed in. Sparkling. The men in their cleverly
casual clothes – bought with the aged look built in. Dressing
down, of course. While I, in my suit, was dressed up. It
defined my inferior status in our relationship rather well,
instantly putting me ill-at-ease through the ensuing ritual of
jokes, compliments and cheek-pecking.

'Hello, Steve. You're looking well . . . rounded!'

'Hi.'

'How's the teaching? Going?'

'Fine.'

'Nice to see you, love.'

My hand was shaken, discarded; my cheek touched

cheeks. And I was promptly ignored.

When, all hostly, I asked what they'd like to drink, they barely interrupted their instant animation to answer; and made me feel like a waiter as I served them. Undeterred, though, I poured myself a big gin and joined their group – or rather, stood beside it as it rattled on its witty way.

I felt about as included as an undertaker at a birthday party.

I tried. Occasionally interjected a 'really!'. But it was pointless. I wasn't one of this lot and the most useful thing I could do was get them another drink. Which I did. With at least some sense of purpose. Everyone knows the feeling of not belonging, but it's strange to experience it in your own home. And the funny thing was, though I tried to put the blame on these friends of Claire's, I could see they were simply people – not that much worse than anyone else. And, much as I disliked them, I could not help but feel that the thing out of place and wrong here was me.

Then Claire gave me her come-and-be-useful-for-once-in-your-life look. Mumbling 'excuse-me' to unlistening ears, I went through to the kitchen.

She'd really done them proud. There was a joint in the oven – beef. She took it out and put it on a carving dish and I took that – and nearly dropped the damn thing. It weighed like cement. Grunting, I got it up to the dining-room, dumped it on the sideboard. I found I was sweating from the strain of carrying – what? A few pounds of meat. I leaned against the sideboard, getting my breath back – and as unsettled as shit.

They jingled in then, with cries of 'Oooh – beef!' – which I'm sure they fed their cats – and I pulled myself together and started to carve. Luckily, we'd just bought a 'Kitchen Devil' (claimed to be the sharpest knife in the world) and, despite my strangely enfeebled condition, it floated through the meat, and I had to watch I didn't slice the sideboard the other side.

But I did less well with the wine.

It was a good bottle of French stuff one of them had brought. I got the corkscrew in – and that in itself was a problem – and knew, almost at once, I wasn't going to be able to get it out. I really wanted to. I gripped the bottle between my knees and for maybe a minute heaved – heaved till I thought the veins in my face would burst and my eyes pop out on the floor. The cork didn't budge. I looked up over it and saw Roger Walsh observing me.

'Shall I have a go?' he asked solicitously.

I handed him the bottle. 'Do.'

And the muscular little bastard didn't even bother to rise from his chair; just took the bottle sitting there and, with no sign of exertion, whipped out the cork.

He handed the thing back to me without comment, clearly trying not to look superior. And everyone else, who had momentarily stopped talking to watch, started again. I went round the table, pouring. 'Poor Claire,' you could almost hear them thinking, 'Her husband can't even open the wine!'

Trying not to feel the idiot I knew I was, I sat down and started to eat.

I wasn't hungry. But, Hitch, I was thirsty and I kept that wine going round and soon moved on to another bottle; and there wasn't any shame involved in this one, because it was one of ours: your genuine dago red, with a plastic flip-top. And so – with all my pouring and more carving and generally waitering – which I do rather well – and what with having quite a few drinks, I managed to plug through a good way of that dinner without feeling too much out of things.

When I'd finished the third bottle, though, it seemed to me time I joined in more.

Old Sandy right next to me didn't look so bad after what I'd been pouring down, and I started talking to her and it seemed I had her attention – till she suddenly spoke right across me to Claire, on the other side of the table. Then I noticed my darling wife signalling me to clear the plates, so I did and took them to the kitchen and brought back the dessert. It was a sort of blancmange – and I had the urge to plump it right in the blond-god face of Roger Walsh and, though of course I did nothing of the sort, the notion amused me as I went about my servile task: 'Oh – Stephen! Yes . . . well, he's frightfully good, really. So useful round the house, my dear . . .'

I sat down.

I sank into isolation.

The evening flowed on and about me.

And I wasn't even a piece of driftwood caught up in it, just a cloud floating somewhere nearby – and all the time evaporating and losing substance. The more I sat there, the more I drank, the more I tried to follow their conversation, the more the lack of contact intensified – till my eyes began to unfocus, my ears. And I felt my exclusion was so total, I was being pushed into another dimension.

I had to assert my identity.

I turned to Sandra beside me. She was talking across the table to Martin. The side of her face was turned to me and, in the light brown hair above her ear, I thought I detected a boil. I studied that and strips of her conversation reached me. Usual politics. I tossed in some remark of my own then, but they paid no attention. It's sort of disconcerting that – when people do that. Especially at your own table. It makes you feel a schmuck.

'I think the National Front should form the next government,' I declared – determined to provoke my way into their conversation.

No response.

'They ought to send all the blacks back!' I said this loud. A remark so objectionable I thought it had to bring some reaction. It didn't.

I felt futile. I'd tried agreement, tried two of the more obnoxious statements I could think of. No-one took any notice . . .

'Hang the bastards – that's the answer!'

Opposite me, Martin waved his hand slightly in the middle of a sentence – rather as one would to brush off a fly.

For a moment then I wondered if it was all some elaborate ploy – this treating me as if I weren't there – but decided no. They really were oblivious of me. Perhaps a more confident man might have found the phenomenon interesting, but I felt damn near destroyed. I had a sort of pathetic half desire to jump up on the table and do a Cossack dance on their plates. Instead, I put a hand on Sandra's thigh.

When that produced no reaction, I made a final attempt: 'I want to fuck you,' I whispered in her ear.

She nodded casually. But I believe her nod was agreement

with some statement of Martin's. In any event, it was all I got.

When I was up at Oxford, a man had given a party and, when nobody came, had hanged himself. I understood why now.

I took my hand off Sandra's thigh, sat back. I poured myself another drink; cradling it, tilted back my chair and looked at the ceiling. There wasn't much to see there. I drank the wine. Looked at Claire's friends. They surely liked to talk. I thought of pouring myself more wine, but instead, leaning heavily on the table, got up and noisily pushed back my chair; and, of course, nobody looked at me then either.

Backing from the table, I studied them all a second, then turned and walked out. I walked steady and held my shoulders back but, you know Hitch, for the second time that day I absurdly felt I wanted to cry. And it wouldn't have mattered if I had.

Because I'm quite sure nobody saw me go.

# CHAPTER SEVEN

*'Now not even the angels in heaven above,*
*Nor the demons down under the sea,*
*Can keep me away*
*From my meeting someday*
*With . . .'*
No!

Enough singing. And why should I feel like singing now, anyway? Now, of all times? Not because I'm in any way cr . . .

There had been faces, you see.

Pale legions of faces, tiered one above the other all through that Friday night. The faces were almost all eyes. Hungry, shark-grey eyes. Watching. Waiting . . .

When they finally dissolved me through to grey Saturday, they turned into Claire's brown eyes staring open on the pillow beside me, little more than a foot away in the bed.

She was looking straight at me – unfocussed and not seeing. I studied her face, but even relaxed the lines in it were set and I found it loveless. I think I sighed then, and my not-so-fresh morning breath blew up her nostrils, because with a sudden frown of distaste she turned away onto her other side.

Somehow that pleased me. 'Enjoy your evening?' I asked.

'Yes. I did, thank you,' she answered. Surprisingly. But that was all.

No questions as to me. Ah, Hitch, the loving dialogue between a man and wife! You know, though, I was smiling as I kicked back the burden of blankets Claire had heaped on the bed. Yes, whatever else you may think about me then, I showed style. I was a man in a paper barrel going over Niagara, yet I whistled as I went through to my dressing-room. And, after wrestling open a drawer, which seemed to have warped in the night, and into jeans Claire had somehow made stiff as boards, I bounced down the stairs still whistling.

Definite style.

Downstairs was littered, stale-smelling, morning-after – which I cheerfully ignored, and went through to the kitchen and started a boil-up. I was ravenous, and not put off by the fact that, taking my three eggs from the pot, they weighed like marble and not your anaemic battery whites. They tasted fine. Gulping them down, I added my shells and dish to the mess in the sink, and went out.

It was good to be out, as if shutting the door was somehow shutting Claire and the . . . problem . . . behind me. I strode off purposefully, was at the junction of Penzance Place and Princedale Road before I realised I had no idea what I intended to do.

Now, I don't know what Tokyo has to offer on a Saturday, but London's got every conceivable entertainment, museum, art gallery, shop, society . . . on a Saturday, for instance the British Unidentified Flying Object Association meets. So too does the Cactus and Succulent Society. But, as at that time I happened to be outside the 'Prince of Wales', I went in.

It wasn't a pub I normally used and, pushing through the heavily brassed swing door, I found I was the first person there – something I hadn't been in a bar since my Oxford days. It was pleasant. I had uninterrupted views of gleaming Victorian mirror in a central section with bottles behind the saloon bar, the chance to step unobstructed to the polished wood itself. I wasn't sure I felt like drinking this early in the morning, but it was good to have a pub to oneself. Perhaps a half of lager . . .

I went to the bar. There was a man in shirtsleeves there with eyes like ketchup-splattered pinballs – one going one way, one the other. They rolled as I motioned at him, and then his shoulders rolled after them; and he sloped away round the mirrored central section – out of sight.

All right. I wasn't in any rush. I waited for him to return and, when he didn't, tried a throat-clearing sound. That didn't get action either, so I wandered round to the public bar. Poor pinball was probably so hungover, he couldn't face serving till he'd had a hair of the dog . . .

The public bar was also empty. But in a corner was a darts board, with three mangy darts in it round the bullseye. I went and pulled them out, surprised as I did at how firmly they were stuck – and then at how heavy they were. Going back to the eight-foot-six mark, I sighted and threw. But . . . my shot fell so low it missed the board. I compensated with the second dart and just hit this time, but failed to stick.

I paused then. My first two throws had disturbed me. I'd played this game before. A lot. But never this poorly, so I really concentrated on my third shot, and threw hard and hit the board all right – but again did not penetrate, and the dart ended up on the floor.

My performance had been that of a child. Puzzled and uneasy, I went and picked up the darts and examined their points. They were blunt – but what pub darts aren't? Stuff it. I took them in a single hand, jabbed them into the board, and turned to go back to the other bar. As I did, I thought I heard one of the darts fall to the floor behind me. But I did not look back to see.

Wanting a drink now, I re-entered the saloon bar alongside a mob of people who had pushed in from the street. And – I'll be damned if that hungover barman wasn't there like a scalded bunny, asking them what they'd have before their elbows even got to the wood.

I stood and patiently waited my turn.

No sooner had the bartender served the last of that group, however, than a new man appeared on the other side of them and caught his attention. Jesus! Did I need a personality enhancement course, need to do EST, just to get a drink here? There were more people coming in all the time now. Was every damn one of them going to get served before me? Leaning over the bar, I stared fixedly at the bartender, made a commanding gesture at him – but he turned promptly towards a girl who was now beside his last customer.

What the hell was happening here?

Whatever it was, it went on. Another five minutes, as the bar did brisk trade. With growing anger I realised that the man had to be doing this to me on purpose, had to be. Someone my size and weight is unignorable when he's leaning half over a bar and waving big-fingered hands at you. I tell you, by this time, I was ready to wrap those fingers round that twerp's throat.

But then, unsummoned, another barman appeared in front of me and absurdly asked, 'You being served?'

And so, in the end, I got my drink.

My god, what aggravation over a pint! I took it to a table and sat there and supped. You get a mixed bag in that pub and over my lager I watched it. It came in waves: the donkey-jacket brigade from a local building site; then your middle classes, recently colonising the area and dressing to look like workers – but, with their soft hands and obliging faces, not making it; then the gay lot, some with earrings, others more discreet; and finally, one misplaced punk with spiked up orange hair, and a padlock on the fly of his jeans.

I sat watching.

Reflecting. And I thought, I don't fit here. Don't know these people, have no slot among them.

I went up to the bar again; positioned myself among a group intent on more drinks, was carried through with them to the action and – by shoving my empty tankard in front of the barman's nose – got it. I took the drink back to the table. A man and woman had also settled there now, but my place was still free and, nodding to the newcomers, I sat back.

And so slipped into my second pint.

Drinking it was a falling into myself. The more I sat and watched the aliveness of the other drinkers, the less I felt substantial. It was a fading away. And the beer must have really affected me. For, before I'd even finished that second pint, I found myself dabbling with a beer puddle on the table – and it seemed to me I could touch the liquid, move my finger across it, and not disturb its surface . . .

A man sat down on my lap.

A bundle of bristles with the smell of a rotten beer barrel, he suddenly flumped down on me – then with a grunt of shock stumbled back to his feet, as I instinctively jerked and heaved him off.

He stood, swaying a little, and glowered down at me.

Outraged. As if I were somehow responsible, had pulled one on him. After a second he grunted, 'Whatcha doin there?'

'I'm *sitting* here.'

He looked at me a moment as if deciding whether or not to make anything more of it, and I rather hoped he would. Then he shook his head and, mumbling something foul beneath his breath, turned away.

Ruffled and embarrassed by the incident, I stared after him – and met the eyes of a girl at a nearby table. She was giggling. She turned away, when she saw me looking at her. At which point, I'd had enough. I drained my pint, squadged the tankard firmly into the strangely viscous puddle on the table, and got up and pushed my way out.

It was raining hard and cold now; and with head lowered and hands in pockets, I headed home.

I was walking quickly and can't have been looking where I was going. Just outside the Islamic Association in Penzance Place I cannoned into someone, lost my footing on the wet pavement, and went sprawling into the gutter.

I wasn't hurt. I got up, even as the man I'd collided with – who didn't seem to have budged – was extending a hand to help me. He was an Arab. In a white Yemeni robe. He apologised profusely in excellent English, and I said, no – it was entirely my fault – and so we bowed to each other and parted. At the steps of my building, I turned and watched his retreating back.

I am six feet tall. I weigh sixteen stone. The man who had knocked me down was the width and height of a rake – perhaps all of five-feet-two.

God, they must breed them tough in the desert, I thought inanely; and went into my building and started up the stairs. As I did, I saw my trousers were torn. I felt a sort of despair when I saw that. Imagine! There was a time when something as insignificant as torn trousers actually mattered! How far away that seems from now . . .

But, to continue . . . I went on up to the flat. Carried on directly up to the bathroom – went in.

Claire was there. Lying on the floor.

Naked. On her back, her hands between her legs.

I stood. Gaped. I believe mumbled 'sorry' then and backed

out. I suppose I was reasonably quick about it; she did not move. Just the look in her eyes changed: from a glaze as I entered, to loathing as I left.

I went downstairs and sat in the kitchen.

The place was just as I'd left it – how long ago now – only hours? And I sat among the pots and dirty dishes, disturbed and not understanding any of it. Ignored, sat on, knocked down – now this. Everything was twisting, going strange; the weirdness was piling on top of me, accelerating . . .

And I couldn't fathom a single part of it.

After a while I got up and started in on the dirty dishes. It was all a bit much, you see. My mind could discern no pattern in it. So I just washed up, until . . . even the plates seemed to become a part of this goddamn day – slipping and straining against my hands, like slimy crustacea . . .

Screw it.

I let the dish I was attempting to dry squirm through my fingers, to smash on the tile floor – and left it there in pieces and went out.

I came here to the drawing-room, and stood at the windows watching the rain beat at the remaining leaves on the chestnuts outside. It was a better sight than dishes.

Some time later, I was aware of Claire in the room behind me.

How long had she been there? I could feel her eyes on my back and wondered whether to turn and face her, and was aware that she'd stand there silently waiting – forever if necessary – till I did.

So I turned.

At once she spat at me, 'Haven't you any decency at all?'

'I said I was sorry.'

'You know very well what I mean: creeping up on me like – like – some Peeping Tom!'

I'd had enough of everything by then. Perhaps I should have been grateful for Claire chewing me out – it was a form of communication – but I wasn't.

'Look,' I told her brutally, 'You want to lie on the floor and play with yourself, lock the door.'

She stared at me. Her eyes – which aren't very big – went huge and I wouldn't have believed they were capable of such expression. Her face inflated, like the head of a spitting cobra. It was ugly, frightening – and I think if she'd had a weapon then, she might well have used it on me. But she didn't and, perhaps from the frustration of that, her eyes filled with tears.

'You filthy scum!'

And she turned and darted out of the room; and seconds later I heard the front door slam.

I found I was shaking.

I went and got a beer from the fridge and wrestled off the ring and had a long swallow – and then raced off the rest of the can. It helped. I was calmer. I swept the broken plate from the floor and made myself finish the washing up. I thought about lunch, but decided on another drink and took a six-pack to the drawing-room, and turned on the tele.

There was some racing on. I lay back on the sofa and watched it, backing losers in my mind and drinking more – and gradually began to enjoy myself. The tele was companionable. I worked my way through the six-pack; made a pleasing semicircle of ring-tops and empty cans on the carpet. And after a while, fell asleep.

Somewhere round four o'clock a siren wailed, mournful and continuous, and half woke me. Dopily I wondered if it could be an air-raid warning and the start of World War Three at last – and thought how simple that would make things. But no bombs fell; after some minutes the siren stopped; and I went back to sleep.

It was dark when I woke.

On the set, an elderly woman was laughing hysterically at her efforts to decorate a cake with icing sugar. I got up and turned the thing off. I had a headache. I listened in the vacuum left by the silenced tele, but there was no sound of Claire. I stood. At a loose end and perhaps still a little drunk, because the next thing I did was pick up the empty beer cans and see if I could lob them across the room into the waste basket – and each time I had a shot I told myself 'If this goes in, everything's going to be all right.'

Very few of the cans went in.

I abandoned the game. It was a dumb way to seek reassurance and I wasn't even sure what I wanted reassurance about.

Hell!

I started pacing the room. I felt caged, but didn't know why, or by what; or how or where to break out to, even if I could. And where was Claire? It was seven o'clock. I went down to the kitchen, looked for something to eat, saw nothing I fancied – despite the fact that I'd hardly eaten all day.

I did find an almost full whisky bottle, though, and the Scots didn't name the stuff 'water of life' for nothing! It would do a lot more for me than a meal.

'Pleasant dreams?'

I opened my eyes. I was on the sofa, the half emptied bottle on the carpet, Claire standing in the doorway. I sat up with a lurch and tried to shake my head clear and look at her. Her cheeks were flushed; she was grinning; and her eyes were unnaturally bright. As my head cleared, I identified that brightness. It was the sort she used to have long ago – after she and I had made love.

She came into the room and swayed across it, swinging her handbag, like a whore from some old-time French movie; and I realised she was more than a little drunk as well. She sloped back into a chair and dangled her legs out in front of her indecorously; and looked at me with a sort of triumphant mockery – and laughed.

'Had a nice evening?' she asked.

'You clearly have.'

She tittered.

'Where have you been?'

'No-one you know, love,' she giggled.

'Where, I said – not *who*.'

'Ooops! Freudian slip!'

I felt a muddy urge to get up and hit her then, to wipe that stupid sneer from her face – and at the same time felt a pity for her too. Or, rather, a sense of her insignificance. She made a pathetic whore. So I just said, 'goodnight' and rose, and went up to bed.

As soon as I reached the bedroom, however, I realised there was no way I could possibly sleep. I'd been doing that, on and off, for most of the last two days and felt – though hungover – deadly awake now. Who knows, perhaps I had a premonitive sense of urgency too – that I must use this little time I had left. Whyever, I went down to the dining-room (which I use as an occasional office) and got out all the paperwork I'd been putting off – bills, tax returns, business letters, homework – and went through the lot. There was a pile of it. And when I'd finally cleared it, I even wrote to friends abroad I hadn't seen in years. It was almost . . . compulsive. An effort to tidy loose ends.

Rather like Christmas.

Or making a will.

Do you know, Mr H, I found enough work to keep me going right through till dawn? Not bad, eh? Even you diligent Japs can hardly improve on that sort of effort. Indeed, in your particular case, I suspect you're pushed to keep it up for more than an hour. One paltry hour . . . what in Satan's name is that?

Enough.

Time enough for the flowing of semen, the flowing of blood; for decisions, revisions, which a paltry hour will reverse. Only – unlike an Italian tank, there isn't any reverse on my particular track, friend.

No rewind on my lifeline . . .

# CHAPTER EIGHT

Sorry. I didn't mean to start frothing and, don't worry, it's all over now. Done. I'm fine, one hundred percent, laughing. See? No problems. Hee! No problems at all.

Ah yes – the last day of that week. The cross-over. Sunday morning in Saint James's Gardens! Autumn all golden-leaved on the ground and gold haloed brown in the trees, and even that god-forsaken grey Victorian church out there not looking too much like the devil's dong.

I tried to open the drawing-room window and breathe in a bit of it all, but the thing had always been stiff and that morning was impossible. What the hell! I felt cobwebby, but good with it; had a high sense of virtue at all the work I'd done in the night.

Admittedly, I was shagged and for a second considered bed – but then I thought of that room, and that woman in the bed, and they did not invite me. I settled on a bath instead. Though easier decided than done . . .

The bath taps did not want to turn.

I nearly put their spokes through my hand, trying to get the water on. They wouldn't budge. It was only when I thought of hammering them with my shoe, that they finally condescended to. And even then did so like setting cement.

Funny how inanimate things can take against you, isn't it?

As the bath filled, I started taking my clothes off. It's a big bath and Claire had put brown mirror tiling above it as a splashback. Looking in that, you can see in reflection another darker bath, another bathroom. Undressing now, I glanced into that dark mirror.

And saw a man in the bath.

My flesh crawled. I looked at the actual empty bath. Looked back to the mirror. The man had gone.

I stood there, partially undressed, the gooseflesh dying on

my body. The man had been lying half-submerged and supine. His body was very thin. Emaciated, almost a skeleton. But I believe the man had been me.

I tried to peer into the depths of that mirror once more – but it was murking with steam from the tub and there was nothing to be seen.

Not really wanting to, I got into the bath; tried to relax. I couldn't shake the picture of that man. . . the fantasy of a tired mind? Or some glimpse into the future, of a reflection before it was there? Foggily, I wondered if my seeing the man in the mirror made him real. And then I thought – you exist to yourself, but suppose you're only made real by other people seeing you.

If no-one knew or acknowledged you were there, would you then – like that man in the mirror – effectively cease to be?

Looking along my bulk crammed in the bath tub, the speculation faded. I was too tired for it, and clearly there all right. Big and blubbery. Somehow reassured, I let myself sink back in the water and for a long time lay there dozily, till . . . I got the crazy feeling that, if I stayed any longer, the water would set around me like amber round a bug. And I would become that skeleton man.

Silly, isn't it, the little things that buzz in the brain?

I got out quickly and dressed again in my clothes of the day before – jeans, a jersey – and getting them on was even more work than it had been yesterday. The clothes seemed to have got tighter, more constricting. It was absurd.

But clothes don't shrink on your body overnight, and I couldn't avoid seeing that whatever was wrong here had to be wrong with me.

I went out for the Sunday papers.

And you know what I thought, as I walked in that morning's sunshine? I thought of wasting illness. Tropical disease. And of things beyond our science – the dark evil drugs of the Malayan jungles; witch doctor potions, that worked with no more than a scratch, the prick of a long, yellow nailed finger . . .

Lord, what absurdity!

I almost laughed out loud. Almost. But there was no

denying that whatever I attempted to do seemed much more difficult. As if I was somehow diminished. Lessening in my effect on the things around me. Striding out across the square then, it was hard to think of myself as . . . ill. I felt well enough. But perhaps – it wouldn't do me any harm to see a doctor on Monday morning.

And, of course, the moment I made that decision, I felt like a million dollars.

I went across the square and down Addison Avenue to 'Mags', the little newspaper shop at the bottom there. It really was one glorious morning. There were men sweeping up the leaves in the gutters – bet you don't get that on a Sunday in Nagasaki – and the streets were fresh and quiet. It's funny how you remember the inconsequential. I clearly recall a large brown dog that was taking its morning constitutional, all head up and chesty – and unaware of a cat that watched him from beneath a car.

I went into 'Mags'. The crone that runs it was stacking papers, back to the door. 'Morning, sweetheart!' I said, as fresh as a breeze.

She's a human hatchet, that woman, with the sort of face that belongs behind a guillotine – and we'd been having a lovely war for as long as I'd been coming here and leafing through her girlie magazines, and never buying any. Naturally, this Sunday she did not reply, but went on with her business. While I, for my part, started gathering my usual read: *Mirror, People, Express, News of the Screws* . . .

I waved them at her. 'Here we go, sexy!'

She gave no indication she heard that, started walking away, then suddenly appeared to notice me – with a jolt. 'Oh,' she hissed, '*You!*'

'None other!'

I smiled. It always seemed to annoy her when I smiled. I used to spend my time in that shop a-grin like an idiot.

'How'd you get there?' she demanded.

Surprised at this departure from routine, I indicated the door.

'I didn't hear the bell.' She peered suspiciously into my face, as if expecting I was about to cosh her.

'No?'

I glanced at it. A large thing on a metal tong. Directly above the door and bound to ring when it opened. 'Maybe you need a new hearing aid,' I said softly.

'What?'

'Nothing.'

I displayed my papers to her. She took them, carefully checked to see I hadn't hidden any extra inside. Then counted my change with narrowed eyes – eyes she kept on me all the way to the door. I heard the bell ring loudly as it swung to behind me.

I lugged my ton of newsprint home.

It's amazing, the weight of our Sunday's. I was really relieved to be able to drop them at last on the sofa, and drop down beside them for my morning read.

Strangely, though, I didn't have my usual stomach for it.

It was the normal blood and boob mixture: adulteries, orgies, black magic, rape. And murder. There seemed to be many more murders than usual. All of them horrible. Chainsaws were in fashion, and one original thinker had taken his mother out, piece by piece, with a scythe. Normally, I get a certain perverse pleasure reading these grisly tales, but this morning I saw them all too vividly.

And, as I read, began to identify with the killers.

I started seeing myself in their place, and doing it. Even in the story of a deranged youth motivelessly strangling an elderly woman he met in the street, I found I was getting a picture of that aged crone, and me young; and so real was it, I could feel her wrinkly dry flesh beneath my fingers. As I squeezed . . .

I threw down the paper and stood.

I felt nauseous, was sweating slightly. They shouldn't publish that sort of filth. It was disgusting. I went quickly to the kitchen; without even thinking, started preparing breakfast. To take up to Claire in bed . . .

Interesting I should feel the need to do that, eh?

I went to great trouble doing it properly too: laying the tray just so, getting the eggs right, even rustling up an actual linen napkin and squeezing two oranges into juice.

Then I took up the tray. With all the stuff that was on it, that was easier said than done. It was quite some effort getting it up the stairs, and I damn near dropped it, juggling the thing about to open the bedroom door.

Claire was asleep when I went in: sprawled at an angle across that frilly pink bed, with most of the bedclothes off. I put down the tray and inspected her. She looked ... unpretty. Like a straggly white spider. Not that it mattered to me then. I felt a silly inner glow, a sense of virtue at actually bringing the bag her breakfast in bed.

I put her tray on a chair by the side of the bed; then remembered I'd forgotten the papers, and went down and got them and arranged them beside the tray. I checked it all looked good, then drew the curtains.

Claire flinched from the light, moving her head under the covers.

'Morning!' I said cheerfully.

She moved deeper under the bedclothes.

Undeterred, I went on louder, 'It's nearly eleven.'

She was fully awake now, I knew, but lay still – hoping perhaps that I'd go away.

'I brought you breakfast!' I blasted at her.

'Oh, Christ,' she moaned from under her pillow; then rolled onto her back and surfaced, scowling at me, 'What do *you want*?'

'I brought you breakfast.'

She saw the tray. 'Oh!' And then, reluctantly, 'Thank you.'

'My pleasure!' I cleared a chair of her clothes, and sat there, feeling faintly triumphant, and smiled.

She sat up, reached for the orange juice, sipped it and pulled a slight face. Then she smiled at me, a cat's smile. 'There was no need to put yourself out,' she purred. And then came the claws, 'Just because you were so perfectly bloody yesterday.'

And so, in a second, everything was soured.

I looked at her lovelessly. She had that smiling, I-can-see-right-into-your-soul expression – and I had another flash of that vision of throttling. And, even as it twisted in me, I was aware of the pleasure there had been, as my two hands tightened into the throat.

I stared at her. Perhaps my expression was somewhat

unusual. Her smile slipped. But I said nothing. Just got up and walked out.

It was then that I decided to leave.

Right then and for good. Without even packing a case. I'd take her car and just drive away. Anywhere for now. Later, I would return and collect my things. By god, I'd do it!

By the time I'd got down the stairs, my determination was total. I scooped the car keys off the table – where years of training had finally taught Claire to leave them – and went out to the street. It was a good day to get away – to go to the country – a great idea. After a little trouble with the Renault's door, I got in and switched on the ignition.

But I could not get the car into gear.

The clutch had locked almost solid. Trying to depress it was like pushing against a boulder. Using all my force, I could almost get the thing down, but could not hold it there. Not long enough. And though I strained with the strength of both arms, and managed some terrible grindings, I could not engage the gear lever. Not in first, or second . . . nowhere.

I struggled for almost ten minutes, before I turned the ignition off and slumped across the wheel. I felt ready to disintegrate with anger and frustration. How could the car do this to me now?

It was the car, of course. The car. It had to be.

I sat a long time at the wheel, looking out over it and seeing nothing as my anger and frustration turned to self-pity; and then that too washed away – and I finally got out, feeling only numb.

I shut the car door and locked it with care. A nice long walk was what I really wanted, anyway.

That would do me just fine.

# CHAPTER NINE

I walked.

There was a goodness in moving and I swung out, covering distance, not noticing where I was headed, just appreciating the going. At one stage, I thought I might stop for a drink and called in at a pub. But, when I was instantly served, I left. Walking was best, you see.

Though I wasn't conscious of direction, I believe I went west through Shepherd's Bush . . .

After some time footing it, I saw a street bench and sat down. I was a long way from anywhere I knew. I looked at my watch. I'd been walking over an hour. I began to take in my surroundings. This was a weird place to put a bench (and the locals must have thought so, because they'd been exercising their razors and knives on that bench and there wasn't much of it left) a grey, narrow street of small, squashed together, flat-fronted grey houses – that looked to be held up more by grime than any mortar between their flaking brick.

As I caught my breath on that dying bench and took it all in, I was aware that the place had an aroma to its squalor, too: a strangely foreign smell, that suggested places east. It must be some ethnic ghetto. God knows, it was dreary, and I got up and started walking to find my way out.

Only – I couldn't remember exactly how I came to be here and, attempting to backtrack, found I was going deeper in . . .

Rather than improve, the area got worse: the streets narrower, the houses more decrepit – some abandoned, with boarded doors and windows – and I found myself detouring to avoid piles of poorly-bagged refuse on the pavements.

I could smell it as I passed. Some of the bags had split, or been chewed open, and their unsavoury contents were oozing through to the street. I went on, wondering about health risks and who was responsible for such slums. Then I passed one particularly foul pile. And heard squeaking.

I've never been fond of rats, and there was something grotesque about that sound from a jumble of black plastic bags. And yet – against my will, I found myself stopping to stare. The squeaking was coming from a bag near the top of the pile. Something in there was moving under the plastic . . .

Bumping and slithering beneath the shiny black, its shape was that of a severed head.

I don't believe I ran.

But I was quickly well away from there. Only – where? I stopped, looked round, tried to get some sort of bearing. There was no way to: identically horrible houses, a glimpse of glowering sky above them, a street name that meant nothing. I had no way of knowing even which way was north or south. I was lost. Lost somewhere in a city I had lived in for years.

There was nothing to do but keep walking.

I started looking for anything that might direct me as I went, but only became more conscious of the area's squalor. It was oppressive and I legged it a little faster. In the end, I would have to come to a major road, a tube, bus station, people. Because . . . did I tell you? There were no people here. It was like a ghost town.

Hah! Your eyes flicker with disbelief. Such a thing cannot be, you say. And yet, it was. London is not Tokyo. And this was like no London I knew.

I came to a crossroads. The street that ran at right angles looked even more desolate, so I went straight across it. On. And as I walked the pavement echoed emptily, the sky grew even darker – till the feeling came to me that I was walking out of this world.

It was not hard to believe. I had never seen such a foetid slum. The houses were sagging now, their grey exteriors like leperous skin, ready to scab off on top of me. And, Jesus – the smell. So heavy I could taste it, the air in that narrow street reeked of rot, mould, entrails, disintegration.

Of death.

How long had it been since people last lived in these houses? I wondered, hurrying on. There was no smoke from their crumbling chimneys now, no curtains in those of their dusty windows that were not boarded, not even abandoned cars parked outside them.

Yet – beneath the urgent clip of my footfalls, I imagined I could hear soft scurrying, shuffling sounds from within them. And hurrying dead centre in the road between their grim rows, it seemed to me the tarmac I walked on crawled with a film of slime.

I wanted out.

Badly. I went faster – but seemed to make no headway. Normally I have a built-in compass and automatically know more or less where I am, but that was gone; and, with no sense of progress or direction, I began to be afraid. There had been a spate of muggings recently, and you could be carved to pieces here and nobody hear you scream – but that was not what frightened me. It was the irrational, but mounting, sense that I could wander forever in this foul limbo – and never come out.

Until I came out in hell.

Should I stop, try to backtrack, find my way to the rat-infested bag – or continue on? Out of all proportion – but no less real – my fear was building to panic. When I saw an intersection ahead, it was all I could do not to run to it.

I paused there, looked at three identical seeming ways to go. I searched inside me for some sense of direction, found only dread – and then saw a car. Parked in the street to my left, it looked like it might not have been abandoned there. I turned and started towards it – and, as I did, a man came out of a house by the car.

'Hey!' I called out to him.

He didn't hear; was unlocking the car door. I called again, and began to run. But, before I could get to him, he was in the car; and had driven away.

I halted, puffing – but suddenly feeling better. This street was no less sinister, I was no clearer on how to get out of this slum, but the simple fact that I had seen another human being had been amazingly comforting. I realised I'd been over-reacting. I simply had to keep calm, keep going, and eventually I would find my way out. I was bound to.

So I walked on.

The street I was in now was long and curving. About half way down it, I became aware of . . . a soft padding sound, barely audible beneath my footsteps. As if a silent multitude of creatures was stalking behind me – barefoot.

I did not look round; registering that sound, was strangely reluctant to; but after a moment thought, this is silly. There may be someone there I can ask the way. And, though I kept walking, I glanced back over my shoulder.

Even now it is hard to believe, to be sure of, what I saw.

They were coming from the leprous houses: some seventy yards behind me, people, perhaps two dozen of them, dressed in loose everyday casual clothes. From both sides of the street, from the long dead houses, they came in silence, the only sound that faint fleshy rustle, as of bare feet, and for an instant I almost stopped and turned towards them. And yet – even at first glance, at that distance, there was something about them that made me uneasy, that struck me as strange – and I kept walking.

That strangeness? I looked back again. They were coming my way, nearer. I could see their skin was very pale, almost translucent. And, oh Jesus, their faces . . .

Their faces were incomplete.

They were like wan plasticene – that some artist had started to model, and then grown tired of – subtly twisted. And where noses or ears or mouths should have been, was only bland blank skin. Shuffling behind me, their bodies swung with unnatural motion. And I was scared right out of my guts.

I faced forward and walked on as fast as I could. I mustn't run. Mustn't! But all the time my ears strained back. And all the time, fast as I walked, it seemed the scuffing of their so quiet feet on the pavement was getting nearer.

A corner ahead. I snatched a look round as I turned it. They were coming, lurching a little, bodies disjointed, a hideous quality to their gait – and yes, impossibly, they were gaining.

Turning into the next road, I ran.

Unfit though I was, I pelted down that dank street and my

chest started heaving, and I was gasping to breathe, even before I reached the end of it. I forced myself on, turned into another road, ran on down its length, turned again – and four strides into that street, could not go on. Gasping, I came to a halt, hung down my head, tried to draw air through the agony of a stitch in my chest.

Between my sobs for breath I heard that soft sound again.

Straightening, I looked back. To see them round the corner, directly behind me, into my street.

Ah . . .

My friend!

How can I describe what I felt, what I saw then? I did not look for long. I slumped. Back against the wall of a building, and slid down it to the pavement; and I hung my head and screwed shut my eyes and waited – for I do not know what.

But they only passed me. With no attempt at contact. And almost in silence: silent-footed, but with strange faint vocal sounds – not words – more like clicks or mews. They shuffled past. I did not look at them. They did nothing to me. Only when they had gone, did I raise my head and stare at their backs.

Strangely – from behind, they looked like normal people. And then I noticed that, away in front of them at the end of the street, a major artery streamed with cars.

When they were some distance gone, I got up and began to follow.

But they seemed almost to float away down the street in front of me, and there was no question of overtaking them, even had I wanted to . . .

Just as they reached the end of the street, though, they paused and turned – all of them – and looked directly at me with their unfinished faces. And I distinctly heard them laugh. Then one raised a twisted arm and made a gesture to me – and I understood that gesture as clearly as if he had spoken in my brain.

'I'll see you,' he said.

# CHAPTER TEN

I have no memory of how I came home.

I know that I followed the faceless people to the main road. And, standing there, had looked up and down it – and, in all its activity and life, seen no sign of them. After that – I don't know. Perhaps I caught a tube back, a bus, a taxi. I only remember standing outside my door in the mid-afternoon, knowing I had come back from some other world; for a moment feeling a terror that world might have overlapped to here – that this might be an identical-seeming, but different number 31, at which someone else now lived . . .

And then I came in and went up, and in the drawing-room saw Claire quietly reading the Sunday papers, and knew that I was truly back. Going upstairs, I took off my jeans and sweater and got into bed and pulled the covers over me.

This was my home.

I was safe here.

I woke on Monday. The bed beside me had been slept in, was empty, Claire gone. I was more hungry than I had ever been in my life, my need for food so demanding it filled the universe. Not bothering with a dressing-gown, I hurried downstairs to the kitchen in my underwear; consumed an entire pack of cornflakes, four eggs, and finally a half-pound pack of bacon.

Only then did I begin to think.

I looked at my watch. It was half-past nine and already I had missed my first class, but that barely concerned me. For, my desperate need for food satisfied now, I was aware that my watch had the weight of a ball and chain on my wrist. And that nothing had changed.

Except me.

I went up to the bathroom and sat on the toilet. Yesterday flooded my mind. Suppressing a sense of dread, I tried to think about it rationally. What had happened to me? Had I found my way into a leper colony? Surely such things no longer existed. Had I then somehow stumbled into another ... dimension? And, oh Jesus, why had those terrible people turned and waved at me with such familiarity?

As if I was one of them.

Feeling suddenly sick, I got up and went to the basin and looked at myself in the mirror above it. All right, my eyes were wild – but nose, ears, mouth were all solidly there. I was no leper, no ... other dimension man. Both my chins needed a shave. I cannot tell you what a relief it was to see that stubbled face I had seen every morning of my adult life, stare back at me – unchanged.

But then, in the mirror, I saw the bath behind me. Its taps. And, feeling sick again, I knew beyond doubt that, if I tried to turn them, I would be unable to. I did not try. I knew I was changed, all right.

And in trouble.

I had to act. Must shave, dress, call school – and definitely see a doctor. Only ... what could I possibly tell him? That I was so weak I was having difficulty doing the simplest of things? Was I weak? I didn't feel it. There was an easy way to find out. I lay on the floor, stretched out. I began to do pressups. I managed fifteen – one more than I'd ever done before in my life.

So.

Sweating, I got to my feet. I was as strong as ever, no doubt of that. The power was there.

Why then could I not apply it? To taps and doors and corkscrews and windows and trays and ... inanimate objects.

That had it in for me.

Imagine! Metal and glass and cork and cloth – all teaming up against me – inanimate things – cabbages and key-rings – all tumbling down upon me in a great garrotting gang. 'Teacher found throttled by his tie' ...

It was insane.

And there was nothing wrong with my brain.

No siree.

Hee-hee!

Not me.

I shaved. I put on a suit. I went downstairs. Thinking was futile. I must act. The only action I could take was to see my doctor. The fart would probably pat me on the head, give me a sugar pill, and say 'next please!'. But I had to do something . . .

I got out my telephone book. The man shared a practice with two other National Health quacks in Notting Hill. They called it a health centre. I dialled.

The telephone was stiff. When I finally managed the number, it was engaged – and I had to sit laboriously dialling for almost fifteen minutes, before I finally got through.

'Notting Hill Health Centre.'

'Good morning, I'd like to make an appointment to see . . .'

'Health Centre!'

'Hello?' I yelled.

'Hello?' they replied, 'Is anyone there?'

'*Yes!* I'd like . . .'

The line went dead.

I dialled back. They were engaged again. Jesus, I thought, how typical. You finally come to a difficult decision – and some petty detail prevents you carrying it through. Ah, the little things! That's what grinds you away in the end. Take my advice, friend – when you go, do it fast.

Unable to get through on the telephone, I had no option now but to turn up at the centre and wait in line till a doctor was available. Which could well mean waiting for hours. Hell! To play safe, I'd have to tell school I was going to miss yet another day. I rang and got straight through – which shows the relative importance people attach to medicine and education – the fools! What do doctors know? They're no better than mechanics, not understanding the machines they tinker with, and which – despite their meddling – inevitably fail in the end.

Remembering my trouble with the health centre, I bellowed down the line this time. Getting through to the school secretary, I apologised for still being ill and promised to be in tomorrow.

'You sure you'll be fit then?' she asked, 'You sound . . . terribly faint.'

'It's the line,' I yelled, 'I'll be okay tomorrow.'

'All right. But do stay in bed if you don't feel up to it.'

We said goodbye, and I hung up feeling lousy. Other teachers would have to sacrifice free periods to sit in on my classes – and free periods were gold. I was really landing them in it. Because of fantasies, some voice in my mind said, but I sneered it down. Fantasies? Okay, take this for a fantasy – and I went and tried to open the window and couldn't, and then tried to lift a corner of the sofa and couldn't do that either. So much for fantasies, mate, I told the voice; and took my mac and headed out.

But at the front door, I paused. Should I leave a note for Claire, to say where I was going? I had a sudden irrational fear, you see, that something might happen to me out there, that I might get sick or even die, die alone. But then I reflected that what would be, would be – and that I'd be no less alone, even if Claire were with me.

God, the streets of London can be desolate in the rain.

Maybe it's the greyness, the slick concrete gulches, the little black bugs of people with their wings wrapped round themselves. There's something about the way people huddle in the rain, curling in on themselves, that emphasises their aloneness. I really felt that, going off to the clinic, a shell in the street, an empty carton on the bus. Identityless.

But the health centre was worse.

It made you feel ill, just being there. A dismal place of potted plants, faded leatherette benches, torn year-old magazines – where many of the clientele looked like they'd come some while too late. And belonged in the undertaker's. Those who were still moving included a screaming Pakistani child, who along with three siblings crawled over its pregnant mother; and a man in a crumpled pinstripe, who kept saying to no-one, 'When is it coming? When is it coming?' And I'm sure meant the end of the world.

There was also a receptionist with a face as quietly expectant as a vulture. I reported to her. With obvious pleasure she said I was in for a very long wait.

Well, I sat there. And I read the ancient Sunday supplements and watched the Paki kid wet itself, and tried to avoid the desperately searching eyes of the muttering man in the pinstripe – and I saw that if I wasn't already crazy, this would make me so. Watching the total lack of concern in one doctor's face, as a palsied man in a wheelchair was pushed through to him, I realised what shits the medics were, too. And that it would mean nothing to them to have me certified . . .

Despite that, I stuck it out there some time.

People came. People went. I stayed unnoticed. With a sort of half-amusement, I wondered – if I were to die and rot here – if anyone would come and sweep away my bones. In the end, I couldn't take any more. I got up and left. I'm not sure but, ironically, I think I heard them calling my name as the door swung to behind me.

So – where do you go when you're suddenly off work and alone, as I was then?

Not to the place you sleep at. To the museums or galleries? Or up west, where the lights are and the crowds? Right! That was the answer for my day: if I were going to play truant, I'd do it like any other child, and have a good time. Yes. 'Have me a time with a poor man's lady – hitching on a twilight train – ain't nothing here that I care – to take along – maybe a song . . .'

What a voice!

I went up to Leicester Square and tried to amuse myself in an amusement arcade.

It was gloomier than the health centre.

There's a perversity about our language. The health centre was packed with the sick. The amusement arcade with the bored – people sheltering from the rain, a funfair of people not having any. No-one smiled, spoke to anyone else. The space invader and pinball tables were tatty, jerked at by men so grimly, you sensed what they'd really like to have done was attack them with an axe.

I attempted a couple of games, but the things were to hell, their buttons so sluggish I had to push like crazy to get them to work and, even then, they had a time lag – so I was shooting at things after they'd gone. Then I ran out of change and went to get more at the booth, and the man behind it was so immersed in his paperback that, though I spoke to him twice, he didn't look up. At which point, I ceased to bother and left.

I wandered up into Soho.

I hadn't been this way for ages but, despite recent clean-up campaigns, it didn't seem to have changed much. Less bum and boob in the sex shop windows perhaps, but, the same sort of blatant titles in the blue film clubs, the same con – fraudulent entry-tickets to a world that I doubted existed anywhere. And I'm sure as hell didn't there.

For a moment I had a crazy notion of going to a strip show – I hadn't done anything like that since I'd got married – but wasn't really keen. And then I had a vision of being recognised and that somehow causing a scandal. News of the Screws style: 'Girl's schoolteacher in sex probe ... Master Molester ... Flashing his mackintosh, Stephen Clements denied today ...'

No.

I had troubles enough without that. And I suppose my face showed what I was thinking. Certainly, walking along Old Compton Street, I was the one man the strip club touts in their doorways failed to treat to the 'show's on now, guv' they gave every other bloke who passed.

I went to a perfectly normal cinema. It was showing a 'comedy', about a mob of detectives trying to solve some ludicrous murder. Not that I laughed. Through the film's first five minutes, I could not shake from my mind the expression of the girl who sold me my ticket. I'd been forced to interrupt a conversation she'd been having with someone inside her booth, by rapping on the glass. She'd looked round – and I'm sure she'd never seen me before; I certainly don't remember ever meeting her – but, as I slid my money forward and asked for a ticket, she stared at me with the shocked expression of someone suddenly encountering an ancient acquaintance come back from the dead.

I tried to concentrate on the film. But, god, it was tedious. The sort of film that should carry a government health warning: 'Danger – boredom can seriously damage your health.' After twenty minutes, I couldn't take any more and walked out.

Boy, was I having fun!

Fun.

And then, perhaps because I was standing in a street suggestive of pleasures of the flesh, or perhaps for some deeper reason, I thought of Linda Durnell – and even as I did, found myself walking towards Piccadilly tube station. It was just four o'clock. I was four stops away from school. I could make it in time to catch her coming out at 4:30. The decision sprang to my mind fully formed. Bugger whether it was right or wrong, she'd been asking for it, she'd get it. It was just what I needed, what I had to do.

I got to school at 4:27.

Feeling furtive and guilty, but strangely excited, I took up position in a doorway on the other side of the street. I did not want to be seen by anyone in authority. I was meant to be ill. Instead, I was lurking, intent on fornication with one of my pupils. By god, it was depraved.

And erotic.

The first kids emerged at precisely 4:31. Parents come to collect them were causing a traffic jam in the road. Unseen, I watched from my doorway as more children began to stream out, get into cars, walk in chattering groups down the street. My plan was simple: Linda had said she lived nearby, would therefore walk home. Whichever way she went, I would follow, bump into her as if by accident; then ask her if she still wanted help with her Shakespeare. . .

There she was! Coming down the steps, full hips swaying, the thrust of her breasts a wonder even from here. Now she was looking to cross the road. She was headed directly my way. I watched her cross, a male driver breaking and holding up traffic to let her. Any second now . . .

When she was just a few yards away, I stepped out in front of her. 'Hello,' I smiled.

Tossing back her honey-blonde hair, eyes fixed ahead, she walked straight past me. Cutting me dead.

Stunned, I just stood there, watched her sway on without even altering pace. I did not follow.

Then the anger came. Goddamn the cock-teasing bitch. Leading me on for so long, then . . . she needed a bloody good kick up the arse! And so did I for being taken in by her.

Seeing a passing taxi, I waved at it angrily, but it kept going. Screw it. I walked back to the tube – from which, duly mauled, I was finally regurgitated thirty minutes later at Holland Park.

Home again.

Home, James, don't spare the horses!

Huh.

Do what you like to the goddamn horses. Spare ME. *Lente currite, noctis equui*! That's Latin, means – run slowly, horses of the night. It's from Marlowe's *Doctor Faustus*, just before the Devil comes. Appropriate? God knows. But don't let anyone tell you education hasn't its uses.

I mean . . .

I don't know what I mean.

My mighty education was good enough that night to get me home on the tube. I cleverly knew how to put the key in the flat door and, stiff though it was, make the lock turn – and then, my god how brilliant, I was able to call out, 'Hi – I'm back!' – and even to my ears it sounded as forsaken as the bleat of a lamb in the desert – and quite as clever and unheard. By Claire there, god bless you Claire, who did not look round from the kitchen as I passed.

Just a peep and a squeak away from the funny farm, I went up the stairs, desperately, bitterly caged in on myself – and, you know, that moment shuffling up the haircord, I think was the first time I thought about it outright.

Seriously thought about taking a hammer and beating out Claire's brains.

# CHAPTER ELEVEN

Trying to make my mind a blank, I stood at the drawing-room windows and looked out into the night. The nearest street lamp wasn't working and the window was faintly reflective, showing me a ghost shape of myself – a big hunched man, staring out into darkness.

I could also see a little way into the gardens, could just see the leaves on the grass by their railings. As I watched, they began to move. Wind, of course – yet it seemed to me then that those leaves were moving of their own accord, individually, starting to crawl forward across the grass, then the pavement, towards me. As if each leaf was some wrinkled, living thing.

I turned away, poured a whisky, scanned the *Radio Times*, sipped my drink, took it for a walk round the room. I was in a bad way: badly needed to talk to someone as frankly as I'm talking to you now. Someone who wouldn't scoff, when I told them that everything in my world was changing horribly . . .

I needed a friend.

I had had several close friends when I'd come down from Oxford; but two had gone abroad and I'd gradually lost touch with the others, and now did not know where they lived – or even if they were still alive. Still, there were masses of other people I knew. Hundreds. There had to be. I went to the desk, got out my address book, looked through it. There were plenty of names there, all right, many acquaintances. But none of them a friend I could turn to now.

I was alone.

I poured another drink and stood staring, sightless, at the room. It was crazy, there had to be *someone*. I supped my drink. I thought. Of course, there were people – most of the other teachers at school, for a start. You couldn't exactly pour out your heart to them, but at least you could have some sort of dialogue, if only about the kids. Which would be fine for tomorrow.

But I needed help tonight.

I went down to the kitchen; looked at Claire cooking; and, after I'd stood and watched her a while, went away.

Back in the drawing-room, I poured another large drink and was aware that once again I was getting plastered. It wasn't helping. I had to break out of this membrane of alienation, of loneliness. Just a voice on the telephone . . .

The Samaritans!

They're the organisation that helps people at the end of the road: alcoholics, would-be suicides . . . The very thought of calling them shook me. It was an admission that my situation was desperate, much more so than I wanted to believe. But then I began to rationalise, and decided that wasn't necessarily true: one needn't be at the very end of your tether just to want some conversation – and what was so drastic about talking to a well-intentioned voice on the other end of a phone? Hell, that's what those people were there for!

Shutting the door, so Claire couldn't hear me, I got their number from the telephone directory and dialled it.

It rang. Quite a while, and I was on the point of hanging up when a male voice answered: 'Hello?'

The voice was dry, dusty; and, though very faint, as if coming from some place far away, had a curiously penetrating quality that made me uneasy – and I realised I did not know what to say.

'We're glad you called.'

'Uh . . .' was all I could manage.

But the rustling dry voice went on, 'You must come to us!'

'What?'

'Or – shall we come to you?'

'Look . . .'

'There is no way you can resist.'

The voice was a snake on sand – obscene – and it chilled me. 'What the . . .'

But again it cut me off. 'It is only a question of time.'

'Who is this?'

'There is nothing you can do.'

'What the hell are you on about?'

'We're waiting, St . . .' The word deteriorated into a hiss – and the line burred, dead.

Slowly, I replaced the receiver. Stunned – then trying to think back over the conversation. It had started like some standardised spiel – but then gone increasingly . . . crazy. There was no way that could have been The Samaritans. Shivering, I recalled the dry malignancy in the voice. I'd got a wrong number, all right. Definitely. Some nutter. But the thing that chilled me to my soul was – that nutter's last word had sounded like my name.

Sick with fear, I sat on the sofa staring into an abyss.

Then the door opened and Claire came in. She surveyed the room and her eyes came to rest on me, and she frowned. I know I was shaking as she looked down at me with her thin-lipped superiority.

To fight back somehow, I snapped, 'What's wrong with *you*?'

She looked at me with disdain. 'Grub's up,' she said, and walked out.

We ate in the kitchen in silence.

Claire read. I drank. Afterwards, we washed up. We did not say a word to each other the entire time. Then I went back to the drawing-room. And like a vast grave, the night gaped open before me.

Not wanting to, I was beginning to understand now, to see the connections . . . No! I would not let myself. I went to a bookshelf, got out a thriller, took it to an armchair and, settling there, tried to read. Forced myself to concentrate. To push down the scum-dripping corpse of realisation that kept trying to surface in my mind.

Where was Claire?

She had not come into the drawing-room. Must have settled in the dining-room. To avoid me. Then I heard her footsteps going up the stairs to bed.

Goodnight, my love. Forever goodnight . . .

A click from the top of the stairs – and the hall was in darkness. I was alone in the only light. It was not bright enough. I got up and turned on every lamp in the room. And then, without questioning why, I shut and I locked the drawing-room door.

If the faceless people had voices, they would sound like that voice on the phone.

I went back and sat in my chair. I picked up the book. Its lines of type squirmed, thin black worms writhing before my eyes. Feeling a scream begin to build in me, I stared them back into words. Made myself read: one word, then another.

And in the street outside I heard the dry slither of the advancing leaves.

*Read*!

Yes. Go on – good – that's good. You're starting to win.

Something was creaking on the stairs.

And suddenly the scream was huge inside me, about to burst out. I must not let it; knew, if I did, I would drown in the sound of that scream through eternity. I rose, threw down my book, strode to the door. But I could not make myself open it. Could not go out from this island of light – to the darkness that waited in the hall.

I went to the sofa, lay along it; turned my face to its back and, curling almost foetal, closed my eyes.

But I could not close my ears.

As I lay there, straining for calm, to clear my mind, to find sleep that would not come, I began to hear a sequence of tiny sounds. As if softly, slowly, everything in the room was realigning.

A faint creak of wood from the armchair, moving, a soft slough of its legs on the carpet; the scuff of frame on plaster, as a painting began to swing on the wall; the ceramic scratch of a vase shifting on a table top; and metal on wood. As the paper knife on the desk began to turn point towards me . . .

Unable to stand it, I spun round on the sofa to see.

Everything was unchanged. The chair, the knife, the vase in their place. The painting hanging motionless, just off the horizontal, as it always had. I began to laugh – with relief and at my foolishness – and settled back on the sofa. Then, about to close my eyes again, I saw the window.

It was not a window any more.

It was a large, black mirror. It did not reflect this room. Eyes wide, flesh crawling, as every hair on my body prickled

with terror, I saw dusty shapes begin to form in the mirror –
and from far down a passage-way leading through them,
heard a soft shuffling . . .

As the unfinished people came.

# CHAPTER TWELVE

I did not let them take me.

I managed to close my eyes. This horror is only in your mind, I told myself. It has to be. And if it is in your mind you can push it out. I pushed, heaved, strained with all my being in struggle within myself to deny them, feeling the cold of their presence now. Hearing their clicks and mews above me – as they laughed.

Then I heard nothing more. When I opened my eyes, it was day. There was sunlight and bird song in the gardens. And I was still here. And I was sane.

Just as I am now.

I rose from the sofa. It was eight o'clock, time for school. I did not think to change the clothes I had slept in, did not think to shave. What mattered was getting there. All normal men go to work, I must go now – not be late.

I wanted to see the children, too. They were good children. Not the sort to give trouble, the kind you read about who even hospitalise their teachers. Not *my* kids! Hell, their idea of mischief was: one Halloween all the first formers – that's girls of ten to eleven – all pretended to be dead when I came into the classroom. Marion Little had tipped me off, though, and I appeared wearing a wizard's hat and carrying a cane.

'One wave of my magic wand across the backside brings a girl to instant life,' I said.

Great giggles.

That's the sort of kids they were. And that morning, heading towards them, I realised how much they mattered to me; that as long as I had this job, however terrible things might be, I was still in touch with, a part of, the real world.

I got to school sharp at five to nine, and went into assembly behind a little gossiping mob.

At nine we had a hymn and a prayer, then a little talk from Mrs Greerson the headmistress, on punctuality. I didn't normally attend assembly, but was glad to be there that day and stand at the back of that brown-linoed, wood-panelled hall, and feel a part of things.

Afterwards, I went and apologised to Mrs Greerson for my absences. Her reaction was strange. She seemed not to hear me at first. Then she peered around her, frowning with a look of vague apprehension and, muttering something I didn't catch, walked off. Normally a woman who looked you straight and deep in the eyes, this behaviour of hers unsettled me badly. And I went to the staff room, collected books, and marched down the endless passage to my classroom with a coldness in my guts that was almost dread.

Heaving shut the classroom door, I went up to my rostrum, put my books on my desk, turned to the class, smiled and said, 'Okay, settle down now!'

But the girls did not respond: milling around, sitting on desk tops, they went on talking to each other in an excited pre-class way – as if I had not yet arrived.

Hah, I thought, game time! Okay, I'd play this one out. I sat down at my desk, folded my arms and, one by one decided simply to stare them into order. I gazed at them stolidly. But it didn't work. In fact, the reverse. They started milling more, talking louder; after five minutes the atmosphere was approaching a party.

'Okay, that's enough!' I said, trying to be firm without raising my voice, 'Let's have some order now.'

That had no effect either.

'*Be quiet*!' I yelled, losing my self-possession and suddenly standing and slamming my hand down on the desk top.

They gave a corporate jerk, surprised, slightly guilty, and came to order and took their places. But there was something about their expressions I didn't like – a cross between sulkiness and excitement. They sat. They looked at me. Some blankly, others as if trying to squint through mist, but all it seemed with a callous, quiet dispassion. As if they knew something about me I didn't, some trick being played on me – a cruel trick they were all a party to.

'Right,' I went on, trying to shake the sensation, 'That's

better.' I looked down at the book on my desk.

Someone tittered.

I jerked up my eyes, but could not spot the culprit.

'Very well,' I went on after a second, 'page one hundred and thiry-three.'

I opened my book, started turning the pages, heard:

'What did he say?'

'Search me.'

'Please sir . . .'

'What did you say, sir?'

'Page a hundred and thirty-three.'

'*What*?'

They were having me on. But why? I looked at them, at their innocent faces. I could not be sure. Deciding to play it straight, I got up to write the number on the blackboard – and the moment my back was turned, the room went vocal.

'What's *that*?'

'It's sir!'

'Piffle.'

'Dummy!'

'Is it?'

Tittering.

I steeled myself and started to write, but they must have soaked the chalk. It had a soggy weight and required extraordinary effort to make any mark on the blackboard. As I laboured over that simple business of writing 133, the voices went on:

'Fat lot you know.'

'Ya boo!'

'It *is*.'

'It's a jelly.'

'A jelly – a jelly!' Voice after voice took it up, 'Smelly old jelly!'

'Okay – *that's enough*!' I turned and sat, noisily thumping my desk top once more. 'Settle *down*!' I determinedly turned to page 133, and so I believe did the children. I looked up and, as they were all more or less in order, decided to continue. We were doing comprehension and my normal practice was to read a piece out, then ask questions and discuss it with the class. 'All right, then,' I said,

and started to read – some poem. I believe it was Tennyson's
*Lotus Eaters*. . .

But no sooner did I begin, than they did.

Just whispering at first, and I went on, trying to blot them
out, hoping they'd quiet. But, cutting through under my
voice, were more sounds: giggling; the snap of a rubber
band, flicking a pellet; the crackle of paper on a packet of
crisps – and the further I went, the louder, more raucous, it
got. A lot of them were whispering now, hardly whispering,
even. It was outright conversation. Animated, amused.
With more and more of the girls joining in.

I couldn't go on.

I looked up and they had sweets and crisps out and were
sitting sideways, generally socialising. Any control I'd had
was gone.

It was a moment teachers nightmare about – the moment
of total ineffectuality – and in that horrible instant, inside a
dizzy disbelief, I noticed I'd brought the chalk back from the
blackboard and laid it on my desk – and I remembered the
way a master at my own junior school had commanded
attention. I picked up the chalk with a furious scream of '*Be
quiet!*' and hurled it at the class.

It came out of my hand with the velocity of a piece of
cotton wool and never even reached the children's desks.
They saw it, though. They began to laugh.

I stood. I am big. I have presence. 'Shut up!' I thundered.

All eyes were on me – bright – and their laughter grew
louder.

'Right! If you don't stop this nonsense now, I'm going to
have you all in after school.'

And then their laughter went mad. It built in them till
they started to roll in their desks.

Laughing at me.

Pointing at me.

Hysterical. Shrieking with a mad delight – and all of it was
turned on me.

My god, Hitch.

I cared for these kids and they were crucifying me; within
minutes had changed from school children to a mob –
cackling, jeering. It was as if I were no longer in front of a
class, but some grotesque exhibit in a freak show. I couldn't

stand it. I would have to strike someone, or leave. I went out of the classroom.

Shrieks of laughter followed me down the passage as I fled.

It begins to get hazy now.

I think I went straight to the staff room. That would have been the place to go. It was there I found myself some time later, sitting in one of its battered armchairs, other teachers talking around me.

Miss Delayo was one, nice Miss Delayo. She teaches history, you see, and lives with her mother. She's a sweet old lady with white hair and big dark lips and very devout, so she loves Italy. And she was talking to Mrs Browning, who's really sympathetic, even though she looks so fierce and frightens the kids with her shaky hands. These very nice ladies were having one of their interminable religious discussions. It was rather cosy, that. Comforting. I sat back and listened.

Miss Delayo was saying, '. . . and what about – "In my Father's House, there are many Mansions"?'

'What about it?'

'It's an obvious pointer to the ecumenical movement!'

I've a good memory, Hitch, haven't I! My senses are keen. Those were their very words. I was listening quite attentively, but it's good to have remembered it all so faithfully. You know, I could even tell you what the staff room smelt like that morning.

It smelt of dust.

'You think so, do you?' Mrs Browning went on, 'Well, that's one interpretation, I suppose. If you ask me, the passage has a far more obvious and straightforward meaning.'

'Namely?'

'That there are different orders of reality – worlds within worlds . . .'

'You mean interdimensionalism?'

'If you care to call it that.'

'Really!'

The two ladies had risen; deep in conversation, were

moving to the door. But I did not hear the rest of what they said. Because I noticed my hand. It was resting along the arm of the chair, perfectly normal. And then – in front of my eyes it suddenly seemed to . . . dissolve.

It flowed into mush. And I could see a mangle of tendons and veins – and heard the blood hiss through them with the sound of a mound of maggots.

I believe that I screamed.

But perhaps those two nice ladies were too old and deaf to hear. They went right on talking, as they walked out of the staff room.

The mind can twist things.

There, out in that busy Knightsbridge street, there wasn't anything wrong with my hands at all. I stared at them, felt one with the other, interlocked my fingers and bent them back till I heard the knuckles crack. Nothing was wrong. Not a thing. It had all been my imagination.

See?

The class must have been too. I mean . . . why should kids behave like that? No reason at all. It felt good knowing it was all just imagination, that none of it had happened. It was like – party time! God, it had been years since I'd been to a party and if I could only have thought of someone to call, I'd have thrown one right then. But, of course, it was getting dark and probably time to go home. It gets dark pretty early in England at this time of the year.

There was only a little gap. Just some hours, you see.

I wanted to go back to school and teach – it was almost a need – but the day was somehow over. Maybe it had been a half day anyhow. I wasn't sure – it sounds silly now – but I couldn't quite remember what day it was. I suppose that's the monotony of the teacher's life for you, huh? But still pretty silly for someone with a mind as clear and sharp as mine.

No matter – I was able to use the time going home to consider what Mrs Delayo had said about different orders of reality, and had some interesting thoughts about that – though I doubt if you'd understand them. You Japs are pretty materialistic, mainly interested in profit and loss. Ah, but there's so much more to the world – the worlds – than that!

I couldn't turn the key in my front door.

When the thing didn't open, I gave it a hard jerk, then a violent wrench. It still didn't budge. Frightened of trying any harder and breaking the key in the lock, I rang the bell – my own doorbell. It made me feel like a stranger, doing that, and for a stupid moment I imagined someone other than Claire might come to the door.

I'm afraid it was her, though. She stood with the thing half open, peering suspiciously into the street.

'Hello,' I said, stepping in.

'Humph.' No stranger would have had so hostile a welcome. She turned her back on me and went up the stairs.

Zip-a-dee do-dah, zip-a-dee day! I heeled the door shut behind me and twinkletoed it up the stairs behind her, slipping on through our flat door like an elf, before she had the chance to slam it in my face – what a salesman I'd have made – the loved one come home!

*The loved one?*

No. No, perhaps not that. I remember that book. 'The Loved One' was dead.

But I . . . I was back. I was good, great. I was gay – that's to say, cheerful. Yes, cheerful. Like dancing. No Claire bitch, no sticking keys, no imagination was a-going to lay one on me. No way. Because, you see, I remember someone saying these things are sent to try us – and by pure addition of all that had been sent to me, that had to mean I was quite a man! Who knows? I didn't, didn't care. I felt good. That alone was a triumph . . .

The whole thing's a goddamn victory story!

Oh

Christ.

Am I rambling?

*Straighten up there!*

Yes, father.

That's better. Now – go on and tell your friend here the really good bit. Ah yes!

So there I am, in the drawing-room on the sofa, with a dirty great grin on my face. There's a near-empty bottle of whisky on the table and I go and pour one – only, that makes it sound easy. In fact, the bottle weighs a ton, and only by sitting on the floor with it gripped between my legs and both hands on the cap, can I manage to unscrew it. But I do, I do! And with two hands I can lift it too, and empty some of the spirit out.

I lug the glass I have filled back to the sofa, and sit there cradling it on my knees. And, in between sips, I know I'm still grinning like a monkey. My mind is a cloud. The sun is on it and the land it wanders over soft. Then a few sharp things begin to come in. Memories. Unlooked for, but filling in gaps and, segment by segment, come back bits of my missing day . . .

Running.

Running from school along Queensgate, turning into Harrington Road, pelting flat out along towards South Ken tube, lungs going, unfit – an unnoticed running man through busy streets, unseen and fleeing what there is no escape from. And all the time as I run, I am keeping, straining, my eyes straight ahead. I am not looking at the things that drive me at the end of my driving arms – my hands.

Into the tube arcade I come, stop. There are lots of people here and my lungs are burning as I gasp and the sweat runs down my head. In automatic reaction I stop, bend, put my hands on my knees and hang down my head to breathe.

And panting there, unnoticed in the crowds, I see now that the hands on my knees are not jelly, but mine.

Then . . . I am pushing at the revolving doors of a department store.

Pushing, but the doors are not moving, hard as I try. Only when a woman pushes from the other side, do they swing and let me in. In. To an emptiness, that place – full though it is of people and merchandise. I wander through it, this vast shell, and the shoppers there assume its emptiness and I want – I want – to drive a bayonet into their bellies; for I'm sure that all that would come out would be air, while the rest of them would woosh down to just skin on my blade point –

a tiny smear of it, not even red.

But I am real as I walk along between counters of women's underwear. I run my hands over counter-displayed necklaces and can feel their gilt beneath my fingers; with only a little exertion move the chains, and watch them respond to my will.

I enter a food hall. There is a pyramid of canned artichoke hearts and I pick up a can at the top, but they have cleverly magnetised it. I lift it only millimetres before it snaps back down from my grasp.

A perfume department next, with dummy-eyed women of complexion so bland they look like they're carved out of soap. Vacantly gazing, fingernail perfect. I go to one, ask for perfume. Not a flicker disturbs her face. Contented at that, I move on. The people here are all mannequins, fantasy figures to suit their products. They move, they suck air a little – sure – but that's illusion. All done with mirrors.

I stand below an escalator and watch the people conveying on up it, and I know how real I am, because I'm afraid.

I fear to step on those moving metal teeth, fear that in their final flattening they will suck in my feet and the rest of me after them. I have the urge to go up though, so I climb the stairs.

A book department. I browse through it, reading the titles, though few mean much to my brain. And, when I try to take one from the shelves, I find they are too closely wedged to remove. A pretty girl sits reading behind a till. I ask her for a title I've seen. I would like to talk to her. But she is deaf, this girl, though she wears no hearing aid – and does not respond.

I drift.

At home as a ghost in a graveyard. Unnoticed by the people there. No eyes catch mine, none of them see . . .

I pass through to the record department. I address a shopper. He does not reply. The department beyond is pianos. I sit at one. A sign says *Do not play* and, though I try, I cannot. The keys are set into steel. I get up and say good day to a man who is tuning another piano, but he can only hear notes of music.

I begin to understand then.

There is a conspiracy. I have been sent to . . . Coventry.

They have enfeebled me, maimed me; are trying to unnotice me out of this world. Into Limbo, where unfinished people . . .

I will not let them. No. I will be seen, I will be. I have an idea.

What an idea! I go to the escalator, stand at the top of the line going down. I wait. I let the inspiration build in me, choosing my moment. A woman appears, an obnoxious, fat little boy in tow. He is whining – a most objectionable sound. This is the one. They step onto the escalator. I am behind them. I raise my foot, thrust it into the brat's fat back.

With all my strength I shove.

He goes, ah how he goes! Shooting out, crashing down end-over-end on the gleaming sharp metal.

I step quietly back. No-one has seen me. But the boy – he has felt my reality. He is at the bottom, his mother wailing over him, on the floor in the middle of a gathering crowd. Even from up here, I can see the blood on his face. He is tossing his head, moaning. Ah, he has something to moan about.

Let them try and ignore me now!

# CHAPTER THIRTEEN

Had I really done that? Had it felt so good?

Sitting on the sofa with my whisky, I found it hard to believe. But I remembered clearly what followed: the pet department, walking up to a beaky salesgirl there . . .

'Do you have any – uh – white mice?' I asked her.

'Mice? Yes, of course. If you'd . . .'

'You heard!'

'You did say white mice?'

'You see me too!'

Oh yeah, she saw me all right. She was frowning now, thinking I was some nutter, not sure how to handle it all, her professional politeness stretched to the limit.

'If you'd like to see what we have . . .'

'No thanks,' I grinned.

I turned. I jiggled away – feeling her eyes, angry and puzzled, on my back. Hah! I had won, broken through. The world was aware of me again – all present and correct.

For then.

But going down in the lift, it started again. I was squashed in a corner, almost suffocated. Though I called out at the first floor to get off there, no-one heard and I was unable to; was kept penned at the back and only barely able to join the exodus at the ground floor, before the people waiting there swept in.

It was back.

Unnoticed once more, trailing-handed over merchandise I could feel, but that didn't feel me, I made my way along the ground floor – and then was back on the darkening street.

Which was where my memories both ended and began.

On the sofa that night, lifting my leaden glass and looking at those missing links of my day, they did not seem enough to fill all the hours. I had come home euphoric. Now that was gone. I thought of the blood on the fat brat's cheeks. Why were they doing this to me? What were they doing? Look at me – I could barely manage this glass.

Oh Jesus.

The relentless progression of it.

The constantly increasing deterioration; fading ... carrying me, brain spinning, powers steadily less. If it continued, I would eventually be ... I would be nothing.

The thought of that gave me sudden vertigo. I felt the atoms in my body, and in the room around me, lurch and interweave – and drawing my knees to my chest, I put my arms around them tight. And held on.

That was steadier.

Till Claire came.

She looked around the room, as if searching for something. Her eyes moved over me, passed on – then returned. They focussed on me with scorn. She was seeing the whisky also.

'You just can't do without it, can you?' she said.

I looked at her.

She looked me back.

'You know,' she sneered, 'The way you ... lean on the bottle, you're no better than a cripple. Pathetic!'

I did not chose to reply just then, but held onto my knees and I believe made a weak negative motion with my head.

'An object of pity,' she went on without any. She shook her head, warmed for her final shot, before making her exit. It was a good one.

'You ought to be in a home,' she said.

I held onto myself a long while. It was a good position. There was comfort in the feel of my body, reassurance. The whole universe might be dissolving, tumbling in and out of itself, but I could feel my arms and my belly and my legs – my flesh. I was there.

I was also weary, terribly weary.

Yet terrified of where sleep could take me. Keeping my eyes from the windows, which could so easily be mirrors now, I fought against a growing fatigue. Feeling myself begin to nod, would clench my teeth, dig my finger nails into my palms till the pain of them revived me.

I would not sleep. Would not.

I was standing in darkness.

The darkness of the blind. A dry buried blackness so absolute, I could not believe that my eyes were open. But even without seeing, I knew that I was no longer in the drawing-room.

The dryness was palpable. I could feel my cheeks begin to contract as it sucked the moisture from them. I gasped in breath. To my nostrils came the smell, the dust, of cremated bones. And even as the sweat of terror broke out on my body, it dried to a film of slime in the aridity of that terrible air.

Then I began to see.

A desert of dusty objects stretched away forever on either side of me, objects endlessly tumbled together and so intertangled that they lost all natural form – an eternity of the discarded artifacts of man.

And I knew that what I had seen before through a black mirror, I was now inside.

Before me was space, a passage leading through the dust-covered lifeless mounds and, though with all my will I tried to fight it, I found myself drawn forward, as the rodent is drawn to the snake, and slowly I walked to the mouth of that passage.

Ahead was dusty darkness. I could not see far. I did not need to. From some time, some place, that I had experienced death, I knew what waited for me down along that endless opening. Then, from the very threshold of hearing came the sound. Almost inaudible. Of deformed naked feet in scores, in hundreds, irregularly dragging, lurching across a dead black earth.

I saw them.

There were so many more. Their forms, shapes, outlines against blackness in distance, silently shambling forwards. The leprous unfinished beings. And I knew this time they would have me. I was in their place.

Yet I went towards them.

Kept on, could not prevent myself. My body was not my own. As I struggled against it, desperately struggled, I kept lurching forward – just as, shuffling and grotesque they came towards me. And now, along with the soft slip of their feet, I heard the hungry gibbering of their clicks and mews, like the scuttling squeak of rats.

A moaning 'No!' bubbled to my lips. Even as my legs moved on of their own accord, my arms began to flail. My hand connected with something, convulsed around it . . .

There was light.

I was in my drawing-room, blinking, cowered in a corner, my hand clutched to a lamp. The muscles in my legs began to judder so violently I could no longer stand and I fell to the floor, shuddered there trembling, aware I had voided myself, feeling my gorge rise.

As I saw on my clothes the fine dust of cremated bones.

# CHAPTER FOURTEEN

How had it happened? How had I come to be there?

The last thing I remembered was huddling on the sofa. The lights had been on then. Claire must have turned them off later, as I slept, leaving me in a darkness that somehow opened the way to that world of horror.

Claire.

The darkness . . .

In the blessed light of morning, I summoned all my strength, got a hammer, and smashed off the stem of the overhead light switch by the door. I broke it in the 'on' position, leaving it immovable.

There would never be night here again.

I felt a little better when I'd done that; better because I'd at least achieved something, taken some action to protect myself; and I determined that, whatever was happening to me, I would fight it. God knows, perhaps some way the process might be reversible.

For a second I again considered getting medical help, but realised it would be futile. What I was suffering was no known disease, and if ever there had been anything our science could have done to help me – which I did not believe there had – that time was already long gone.

Feeling a desperate sense of futility take, and nearly over-whelm me, I strode away from it up to my dressing-room.

I had to cling on.

It took me time, but I managed to open my clothes cup-board and drawers and get out fresh clothes. I was able to put them on. Forcing shirt buttons into their holes with fingers of putty, a strange thought came to me.

Could Claire be in some way responsible?

Could she be feeding me some hallucinogen, a slow-acting poison perhaps, that was steadily, impossibly, turning me into . . . a non-thing? The idea was insane. Yet, as I thought about it, for a second I imagined I could feel an alien substance running in my veins, dissolving me from the inside outwards, and slowly turning me to mush.

I had to get out of here,

I struggled into a jacket, hurried out of my dressing-room. Slap into Claire.

She knocked me back, out of her way, like so much cotton wool; walked on as if there had been no contact. She went into the bathroom, without shutting the door, pulled up her skirt and sat on the toilet – all as unselfconsciously as if she were there alone. She had an almost purring look of contentment in her eyes, and I couldn't bear it. I swung away from the bathroom, pounded down the stairs, kicked and battered my way out of the door, and dashed out – and, though I was not aware of it then, I recall that my jaw hurt from the intensity with which I was grinding my teeth.

Outside in the street, I ran. Across the gardens. From Claire, from myself, from this thing that kept building . . . ran through rain, down Princedale Road, grey and sleek with it and then – I don't know why – was suddenly terrified that the rain was not wetting me, that I was somehow not intercepting it. I stopped. So abruptly I slipped and almost fell. I looked down at my clothes. And I was wet, good and truly wet. It was awful how wet I was – and bloody wonderful.

Briefly then, I believe I realised that my brain was dangling and jerking like a bird-pecked half coconut on a string.

*Oh Mary do not weep for me*
*Oh Mary, just you wait. . .*
No. Not that. Perhaps . . .
*Bury me not on the lone prairie.*
*Bury me here, in S.W.3*
No way. That's even worse. Silly. A far more dignified song is required, something more . . . Japanese? Why not? I don't know anything Japanese. All right, I'll make it up.
*There are bones turned to atoms*
*In the land of the rising sun*

*Where the dust of the dead will beckon*
*And welcome the dead to come.*

No, that's little better, next to useless. I know that. I do.
But . . . when did they ever write a song about anything like
this?

Hang on! What about . . .?

No.

I've forgotten what I was going to think anyway.


I got to school.

Got there – but could not get in. I stood outside the door
and pushed, pushed hard, but surely the thing was locked. It
did not so much as tremble against all my pressure. I could
see through it glass panes, see the kids gathered for assembly
inside the main hall, but I was barred. I tried knocking and
waving to attract their attention, but they were all looking
forward towards Mrs Greerson, speaking there, and did not
see or hear me.

Beaten, and not knowing what to do, I turned away. And
then – there was Linda Durnell, running up the school steps
to the door.

'It's locked,' I told her awkwardly.

She went past me, pushed through the door and went in.

For a moment I stood. Then just before the door could
swing to, I jumped in after her.

Assembly had ended. The children, like so many min-
iature Mongols, were streaming off to their respective
classrooms; and as I stood there, they flowed in blind hordes,
shoving against, around, past, me, and – insanely, horribly –
I imagined through me too.

I felt my guts drain down through my legs to the floor,
rooting me there. I believe I stayed like that some time,
before I finally shook the feeling off. And in that large and
now echoingly vacant hall I knew the loneliness of a man
trapped behind in a football stadium, when all the crowd has
gone home. But I shook myself. Exactly that. I could feel the
jelly sloshing inside my skull. That was how hard I shook
myself, before I moved on.

So I came to the corridor. The one with my classroom.

Already I could see its door was closed, but I tried – I tried – to fight down how that worried me, and for a moment paused. Without knowing why, I knew I shouldn't go on, But I did. I came to the classroom and pushed against its door, and it too did not move. I raised my head then and looked through its panes.

Someone else was taking my class.

It was wrong that, terribly wrong, and I cannot tell you how it scared me. It was as if I suddenly did not belong here, never had. Again I pushed uselessly against the door. I knocked on its panes then, knocked so hard my knuckles hurt, but the only sound they made was a muted slap, like a flabby hand hitting dough. It could not have been heard above that man's voice in the classroom.

Wanting to scream with a desperate frustration, I tried willing him to look at me. It was all I could think to do. I stared at him – concentrated on making him turn towards me – and finally he did. But though he faced me, it was clear he did not see me as I stood outside the classroom and gesticulated at him. There was no change of expression in his face, and a moment later he turned his attention back to the class.

My exclusion was total.

I had no place here. Numbly, I turned, started slowly back. Desolate as the only living being in a world of the dead, I made my way down the empty halls and corridors of dark brown; and this place, that in my mind always rang with activity had the dusty quiet now of a long-abandoned ghost town.

Feeling I was lost in some limbo land between existences, I passed classrooms where I could see life and animation; but, shut out from that life, out here there was nothing. I walked through a void, with only the sound of my footsteps to fill it, the sound of my footsteps walking beside me like a shadow.

I went to the staff room.

As soon as I entered, I sensed something was wrong. The room was . . . subtly changed. The clutter, the pre-war furniture was all the same, and at first I could not see what had altered – but then I looked at my shelf. My things were no longer on it. My pens and papers, my books, all my books, had gone.

And then an ugly realisation began to grow in me and, struggling to suppress it, I went back to the main assembly hall.

I went to the noticeboard. I stared along it, studied the names of every teacher taking every period that week. My name was not among them.

I double-checked through each piece of paper pinned on that board – and it was true, but I could not believe it. My books, my class – now my name – all were gone. Every sign of me here was obliterated. As if I had never been.

Dazed and frightened, I tried to think. I had heard of teachers being dismissed at short notice before – though, god knows, not very often – but this, this was impossible. I spun away from the noticeboard; suddenly angry and trying to stoke that anger, stormed towards Mrs Greerson's office. I wanted an explanation, and it had better be a damned good one!

In the minute or so that it took to reach her office, I almost managed to work myself into a rage. But in all my mental rantings there was one thing I never considered: Mrs Greeson's office had a door.

It was closed when I came to it. I raised a fist to knock – and undersea tentacles of slime began to wave in my belly, as I remembered the sponge-soft sound my knuckles had made on the classroom door.

Sweating, but no longer with anger, I let my arm fall. I stared at the doorknob, a round of white enamel gleaming in the door's dark wood. I stretched out a hand . . . but never touched it; could not try to turn that knob. I did not dare to. Another failure to do something any child can do, would destroy me.

Fists clenched, teeth gnashing, standing outside that door I did not have the courage to see if I could pass, the tears came burning from my eyes. I could not stand it. I turned away and I ran.

The main entrance must have been open. I ran through it and stood on the school steps, turning my head round over

Queensgate right and left, like a hunted thing vainly searching for a bolt hole; and, as I stood there, incredibly I saw John Cunningham.

Like the answer to a prayer.

I hadn't spoken to or seen him in years, yet there he was: turning down from the Cromwell Road and striding towards me. He'd gained weight, lost hair, and his nose had sprouted small florrid veins, but it was John all right. We'd roomed together for a term at Oxford. He did not look as if life had been kind to him since – his suit was tired, his briefcase tatty – yet there was still a defiant sense of the man I had known as with purposeful stride he came down Queensgate, almost level with me now . . .

'John!' I called.

'John Cunningham!' I called out again.

He went on past me, striding on.

For a moment I hesitated, expecting him suddenly to stop, turn back. He didn't – and I ran down the steps, went after him, caught up in just a few strides and clutched at his arm.

Or tried to.

My hand fluffed off it with as little impression as if it had been the wind that plucked at his sleeve.

A man with his mind on things does not notice a gust of wind, and he walked on. And I, of course, just stood there, staring after him, trying to tell myself I'd been mistaken – that he'd never been John Cunningham at all.

I had to be where there were people then.

I started walking. I went up to the six lane width of the Cromwell Road. There were lots of cars there. I watched them pass. I crossed the road, turned right, walked again: towards Knightsbridge, past the vast Romanesque palace of the Natural History Museum, with its terracotta animals and petrified trees. There weren't many people, though: at the corner of Exhibition Road some students coming out of the Imperial College of Science and a party of foreigners being addressed by a guide with a map. No good talking to them, to the foreigners, to the students – to the guide with the map in his hand.

I went on up to where Cromwell and Brompton Roads

join, and on my left was the Oratory – a large baroque Catholic church. The high columned portico of its entrance was open and, for a moment, I paused outside it and actually thought of going in, of finding and talking to a priest. But I've never believed in god, didn't then and – despite all that's happened – do not now. The Devil perhaps, ah yes, that's far more likely!

Wouldn't you say so Claire, my love?

But as for me . . . I wasn't that far gone. Not enough to think some character in a penguin suit could rationalise the insanity of our universe. Oh no, much as I wanted, desperately wanted people – someone, anyone – to talk to, priests are not people, and I passed that place by.

I'm rather proud of that.

Even at that dark hour, at the ending of a world, I did not succumb to superstition. A negative victory perhaps, but a victory in its way nonetheless. Perhaps my only one. But I believe there was a little less ache in me, as I went over the zebra crossing by Brompton Square to 'The Bunch of Grapes' on the other side of the road.

I do not like to remember this: pushing and shoving at the big bright brass handle on one of the doors of that pub, and it not opening; but still trying, not daring to stop for the sudden panic that this was my final handhold; that, if I did not get in, if I let go that brass handle, I would be letting go of existence – and be blown like dust down a tunnel along Knightsbridge, on forever and away.

Then the door flew open; and, like a desperate drunk I lurched in and almost onto the jutting breasts of a frizzy woman who had just unlocked it. What a fool I had been – it was only just opening time!

I regained my balance, said 'hello' to the woman's back, and she disappeared behind a bar.

There's a circle of separate bars, all with elaborately carved wood partitions, in that place and if you get stuck in the wrong one, you can wait forever and not get served; so I moved round to the largest, where it looked like the woman had gone. She had; was polishing a glass there.

'Morning,' I said and, because it had stopped raining, 'Not a bad day!'

112

She put down her glass and walked through to another bar.

The old conspiracy was still going.

The bastards! I remembered what had happened to me in 'The Prince of Wales'. All right, I thought – and went and sat down at a table – if they were going to behave as though I weren't there, I would too. Would sit and enjoy the place, buying nothing, and so get it all for free. When they saw I was doing that, they would come running to hassle me soon enough . . .

So I sat at a table, calmly crossed my legs, stretched out my arms on the table top, linked my fingers and relaxed back facing the bar. This was the answer! I would outstay them at their own game. All day if necessary. And when the big-breasted frizzy woman came back to the bar, I treated her to my broadest smile.

And I sat there.

I kept the smile on. People came in. It's amazing how quickly they start to come once a pub opens, and of course 'The Grapes' has always been popular and quite soon started to fill. And I sat there. Watching the people buying their drinks at the bar; listening to their chatter; smelling the sourness of their beer, their cigarette smoke. I sat there.

The pub got full.

All the time fuller, and I realised my idea was no good. There were far too many people in the way now for anyone to have seen me from the bar. Not that it mattered. I mean – I mean – I seldom drink – and it was far too early in the day for me to want to anyway, why – hardly even lunchtime, I think, and . . . and . . .

I remembered the boy I had kicked down the escalator.

I had been noticed after that.

I got up. I walked to the bar. In the mirror behind it, I could see myself smiling. I found a space between two groups of people and moved into it. I put my hands on the bar, took my weight on them, and vaulted over to the other side.

I looked around. There was only one girl serving in all that space. Deliberately I moved along the row of bottles, using all my strength, forced them off with my arm; hearing them crash to the floor behind me, kept going to the end of the row. Then I made my way back through broken glass and spirits to the place I had jumped in from, and climbed back to the other side of the bar.

That was better! Now I could leave.

I turned for the door, behind me heard raised voices of surprise, of consternation, but I did not bother to look back at them. I'd had my satisfaction. I was cool.

I walked a few paces, and there was a man in front of me. 'Excuse me,' I said.

But despite what I had just done, he still pretended not to notice me and went on talking to a man beside him. I raised my voice and repeated myself – harshly – and when he didn't respond to that, got ready to push him aside . . .

And was savagely shoved in the back.

It became confused then.

People were surging at me from behind, moving onto me from in front, and I was caught between them – caught. Pinned, unable to move, and they kept coming, pressing in on me, constricting me, so that it seemed they were trying to crowd their bodies into the space I already occupied. I felt myself lifted by their mass; helpless, was carried back, forth, across that pub like a powerless piece of weed in the sea.

My head spun. I was suffocating, drowning, being blotted to death. There were men, faces, stubble, sweat smell, constriction. It spun around and in on me, trying to squash me out of existence. I fought. Pushed, swore, yelled against that bedlam, and then suddenly was by the door as it opened – and out in the street.

I took two tottering steps, then sagged against the wall of the pub, gasping for breath and gagging; slowly sank down the wall to the pavement and squatted there – and though it was only midday, I saw night.

The world had gone mad.

That had to be the reason, didn't it? *Didn't it*? It could only be that. It must be. That – or else . . .

The alternative was unthinkable. Yet as I slumped there

on the pavement, I could not keep the hell-vile thought from my mind: the reason no-one recognised my existence was horribly simple. I no longer had any.

I was dead.

# CHAPTER FIFTEEN

There are many forms of fear.

There is the soft breath that touches you to a shiver, in what is near to excitement, and a pleasure. There is the skeleton, ice-tendoned hand which seizes round the heart so hard that feeble gristle can no longer pump. And there is what I felt then.

Terror. So sudden, so absolute, you void yourself – your guts a foetid jelly pouring out down your trembling legs, as the tears from your eyes, the grunts of hysterical laughter from your blubbering mouth.

I tried to stand against it, that midday night, legs jerking, hands clawing to the brick wall at my side. I tried. And all the while, my mind kept saying – *dead*. I had died and somehow, not known and now was forever trapped here, to wander helplessly . . .

NO!

It was impossible. Insane. I *was*. I was here. Was real.

I knew that. I could feel the brick of the wall beneath my fingers. I felt it harder. Harder. Pressing my hands with all my force against that brick, I slowly moved my fingers down it, shredding their skin, leaving the smudge of my blood . . . that was real. I felt the wall. I had left myself on it. I looked at my fingertips – mince raw. I put them to my mouth.

I tasted the sweetness of my blood.

Ah!

Was I not real now?

Just as the wall was real. The pub and its door. But what if I were to push against that door?

It would not move.

And that would prove.

The Devil and the deep blue sea.

I've got . . . I'm not . . .

Not me.

I did not push at the door. I mean – what I mean to say is –
I did not go into the pub. It was far too noisy, too crowded.
Besides – and anyway, as you very well know, I do not like to
drink at lunchtime.

The dead can't drink.

The dead can't think.

The dead cannot even pee.

Nor do they bleed. Whereas I . . . could do all of those
things. They just couldn't do them back to me. No – I – think
– think – think – my brain is gonging, words running wild on
my gob and I gut – gut . . .

# CHAPTER SIXTEEN

I'm sorry – I believe I was telling you something?

Something about myself. Ah yes! That very real, important person. Hah! There's little doubt about my reality now, is there? You might say we've proved it, Claire and I – and, oh yes, you too Hitch. We three!

I was saying – I thought I was dead.

The living dead that walked the ways of Knightsbridge. Ridiculous! But not very funny; not then, not to me.

I went from 'The Bunch of Grapes' towards Harrods. I was a wisp in that busy street and I kept my eyes on the people's faces floating on towards and past me; and there was no acknowledgement of my existence from any of them.

I stopped and looked in a shop window. There were naked dummies in it against a dark background, and I could see myself reflected in there and my reflection was as real as those of the people passing behind me. Perhaps life is all reflection, I thought, perhaps none of us there existed. Inside the window, only the dummies were real.

With a surge of fear then, I saw how like a dark mirror that window was and I spun away from its ghost shapes before other . . . shapes could come. Dead to the world or not, it was certain then that whatever it is that matters inside you, was dying in me: my mind, my soul – an inch-high naked figure gesticulating on ice, shrivelled and numbed cold and jibbering.

I walked up Knightsbridge, crossed the road where it joins Kensington and went through beneath Bowater House, by the Epstein statue there, into Hyde Park. Looking at that straining-winged statue as I passed, it seemed to me to be saying something to me, so I stopped for a moment and studied it – and, though I could not make out what it said, it had a great beauty, and watching it made me want to cry.

I was a mess.

I crossed over Carriage Road and Rotten Row into the park. Did I say it had been raining? The grass was wet and glistening, and scattered with sodden leaves from spikey branched trees, that were mostly dead and bare. It was cold. I walked onto the grass and started across it and it was hard going; the grass was so long it seemed to be reaching to snare my feet. A hundred yards or so in, I stopped and sat on a bench in an open space – and felt the water from all that wet grass seep its way through my now sodden shoes to my feet.

I sat on that park bench, breathing a little; trying just to be. The sky was hard grey. There was a wind and leaves were being eddied, and not very far away some office workers were doggedly playing soccer in what I supposed was their lunch break.

My god, it was all so sad.

I got up to walk away from it, took two steps – and something hurtled at my face. I threw up a hand and ducked. With a swoosh, a pigeon went over my head, so close I felt the wind of its flight on my hair.

A pigeon.

The keenest-eyes of birds, that can spot a piece of bread on the ground from miles. If I had not ducked, it would have flown right into me. A kamikazi flier? An ancient refugee from Hitchcock's *Birds*? I do not think so. I believe it simply did not see me. Was flying about its business as if there were no obstacle there.

If ever I needed proof I had entered the spirit world, I had it now.

I turned back to the bench, sat down again. No man, no man ever, was as alone as I. I sat on the bench there, my friend, and I began to cry.

Pathetic, I know.

It did not last. Remember that, when they take you to the knacker's yard, as they will with us all, when they grind your innards to so much mush. Nothing does. It is the only comfort in our lives.

I wiped the wet from my eyes and used them to see with

again. The soccer players were still there, shouting to each other as they ran, and the wind was taking their words and twisting them to me in snatches. I saw another figure now also: an elderly bent woman slowly approaching across the grass. She wore a long grey coat, moved with small footsteps, holding her head down against the wind – and it bobbed a little as she walked.

I looked at her but did not look at her, if you know what I mean. My eyes went past her to the spaces beyond the trees, to their branches moving thin in the wind. I had things on my mind.

But the elderly woman, by a roundabout route past the soccer players, came up to my bench. And there she decided to sit. On my right. I turned my head and looked at her properly as she did, and she looked my way also; and gave a sort of nod towards me – and smiled.

' 'Ullo,' she said.

I could hardly believe it. She had spoken to me! In a perfectly normal way, as one would to any normal, live, solid, natural human being. Who was *there*. My god, that was gold.

'Hello,' I think I answered.

'Nippy, i'n' it?'

'Yes. Yes, it certainly is!'

I looked at her, beamed at her. She was regarding me with a whiskered, brown, sagging-skinned face – and strangely unfocussed and watery eyes. She was not lovely, but I loved her.

She turned her head slightly sideways and smiled. Her teeth were brown and few. 'You're a nice looking young feller,' she said.

I did not take the words in, but they were music. My hell was over. I wanted to kiss her leathery cheeks. It was maybe the finest moment of my life.

And it was brief.

She looked out away from us both across the park and asked, 'On leave then, are you?'

'What?'

Staring fixedly in front of her with a sort of smile, she continued, 'What lot are you with then?'

'I'm sorry?'

'I know what you're thinking,' she chuckled – and then

turned her head full away from me and spoke directly in the opposite direction – but her words were blown back by the wind:

'What's a nice girl like me doin' in a place like this, eh?'

I know I am slow – it was only then that I felt the first chill.

'Show you then, shall I?' She turned her head forward once more and giggled obscenely, and nudged with her right elbow into space.

Then I saw.

Saw it all: the filth by the side of her mouth; the sores on her neck; that her long grey coat was torn and threadbare and, below the splotched grey stockings beneath it, there was little left of her shoes – and through them protruded scrawny and gangrenous grey-green toes.

'How 'bout some fun, eh?'

I rose from the bench.

'Come on, dearie!' she cackled into space.

She squirmed on the seat, scrunching up her withered body beneath the grey coat and, writhing towards the bench's emptiness, simpered to nothing, 'A nice short time for a quid!'

And she reached across and grabbed the arm of the bench and squeezed it persuasively, and ogled out into space.

I heard someone sob then.

Looking back now, I do not believe it was the woman, the ancient mad harlot plying trade with the ghosts of her past. I do not think it was her. But I turned from the bench to walk away from it and it came with me. Undiminished, the further I went I still heard it.

Sobbing loud, like a soul torn in pieces.

# CHAPTER SEVENTEEN

There's no need to tell an oriental such as yourself that the situation now called for considerable cunning.

There was a horrible conspiracy to render me substance-less as the image of a man on film that was fading, to un-notice me out of the real universe into some leprous dimension of the damned. To defeat it, I would have to move cautiously, cleverly – terribly cleverly. But ah, I would do that. They would not have me. I would outwit them, unravel their conspiracy – destroy them.

First, I must prove to myself, once and forever, that my existence was no illusion. That sounds insane, but when you're up against a thing this vile, you have to start at the start.

Oh yes.

I would prove myself in stages. First to me, then to objects, animals, people. Wherever I failed, I'd have my clues – all the great detectives have to be methodical like that – then I'd follow those clues and – and Sherlock Holmes would have nothing on me!

Who can have nothing on nothing?

Ah!

Think about that one. It'll come to you. It came to me. Oh yeah, it all came to me.

And so – the relentless machinery of my mind grinding fine, I started stage one of the plan. It was easy. I saw I was standing by the Albert Memorial, a monument with steps all around it and Queen Victoria's husband Albert instoned on top, and staring out in eternal boredom at the road. I sat on the steps and stared out too. And though I may have sat like a statue, all the time I was moving. Inside. Examining myself – and I felt real: my heart jigging, brain clicking, blood pounding – everything in me going on. I moved from the inside out. Some time had passed. It was colder. I must have been running recently too because, despite the cold, I was sweating and could smell that sweat as it began to dry. It wasn't a pleasant smell, but it was good and real – the smell of a man alive. I reached down to the step I sat on. It was cold beneath me and my rubbed-raw fingertips could trace the textured grit of the concrete on their new formed scabs. I pressed till those scabs burst open, and again there was blood.

The stuff of life.

I got up and walked out of the park into Kensington Gore. A bus was just pulling away from a stop there and I ran and jumped and caught it. A number fourteen, going east.

It was time for stage two of the plan.

I went to the front of the bus and sat there and naturally the Jamaican conductress never came and asked for my fare, but that was fine, riding free; and I sat there up front right to Piccadilly, sat contentedly all the way. I didn't make any trouble. In fact, I'm pleased to recall that most of the time I had a smile on my face.

I got out by the BL car showrooms, and stood on the pavement looking round for inspiration. I didn't see any and started eastwards along Piccadilly. About half way up it I got tired of that side of the street and crossed over, and a little way on found myself outside Cogswell and Harrison, the gunsmiths.

I stopped and looked in their window. They had an impressive array of shotguns, and it occurred to me that there's something quite attention getting about a man in a city street with a 12-bore in his hands . . .

Without even thinking, I turned my body sideways to the window – and lashed out at it with my foot.

I kicked with all my force and weight, connected with the hard side of my shoe. It was like kicking steel. I bruised the bones in my foot, but did nothing to the window and found myself hopping with pain on the pavement. This was no way to make an impression. Let me try things of flesh. They would be easier, softer . . .

I caught a bus up to Regent's Park and the zoo.

At the zoo, the eyes of the man in the ticket booth went

no higher than the money I pushed in front of them; but he acknowledged that politely enough, saying 'thank you' to it, as he slid me a ticket. With some difficulty then, I made my way through the turnstile. You see why I was here? If animals could perceive me, it would be proof positive that the conspiracy was *human*. If they couldn't ... I pushed the thought aside and went into the first building I came to.

The reptile house.

It is hot and humid in there; and it is dark. You imagine you can smell the scales of the coiled things that lie behind the glass. Crocodiles came first, and alligators, lying in a green half light of glassed-over pens. They were so still they were hard to make out: stone-like, heavy-scaled, their eyes of sparkling saliva, their jagged-toothed jaws open, waiting. No waving or screaming would alter those creatures' stillness. There was only one way to do that, a way I did not fancy. But fortunately, the glass was there – and from this side of it, they remained so motionlessly distant, they might for all I knew have been stuffed.

I moved on to the snakes.

In glass-fronted row after row they lay, twisted and twined on rocks and dead wood, and at times round each other, so intricately that you could not tell where one coiled horror ceased and another began.

In sick fascination, forgetting what I was there for, I wandered from cage to cage, absorbed by the poisonous waiting things inside them. And I had a vision of the day they would all pour forth, these Devil's creatures, and of what they would do.

I watched a Mamba: a lank loop over a long dead branch, its scales a slimy near phosphorescent green. The venom from that snake can kill in seconds, I believe, but cut off behind glass it lay frustrated, quite still . . .

Cut off from the world behind glass – a one way glass, perhaps, like whatever they had spun around me.

There was a cobra in the next-door cage. I went and stood in front of it, and suddenly – it began to move.

Unwinding, stretching, one slithering scaled muscle, it rose. The way a snake moves is magnificent and watching that cobra, only inches from my eyes behind glass, was a horrible joy. It rose. Upright before me. The skin around its head blowing out, it hooded – straight at me, its forked tongue flicking. It was so close I couldn't help stepping back. But I was glad, Hitch, glad. It was aware of me, that vile thing. Of me . . .

Or what stood behind me.

On the other side of the swaying menace of the snake, faintly reflected in the glass that contained it, I saw faces behind me: unfinished faces with gashed mouths, vacant eye sockets, thin vertical holes where their noses should have been. Foully distorted flesh, horribly grimacing, I watched them in the glass and with the chill of death upon me saw their hands reach out. They were hooked into claws, grey-white translucent hands, whose veins I could see through, and, where blood should have run, maggots writhed.

I was near turned to stone with terror, but before those clawing hands could touch me, I managed to turn.

There was nothing there.

Not even people. Oh, there were plenty round the other snakes, but none where I stood here. For a time I stayed frozen, barely noticing that in the cage beside me the cobra was slumping, slithering back to a corner . . .

Oh Jesus, they had come again. In the daytime and in no leper land, but here.

A wave of nausea swept over me; I felt the world shift, my vision haze, and the floor beneath me tremble. I do not recall leaving the reptile house, but when things steadied and came clear again, I was standing outside it, blinking in a thin autumn sun. The cooling sweat on my body came to my nostrils like bile – and close by a hugely fat woman in a billowing blue dress was buying herself and her equally obese daughter ice creams.

What was I doing here?

Running.

No. I remembered my purpose. I had to fight. I remembered my plan. I started walking. Past the armour-plated rhinocerous – useless – then the decaying toothed mass of a hippo, on; purpose recalled and defined, on to the carnivores.

If I put my hand in a lion's cage, I would know.

You've noticed I still have my hand? A fine hand it is too, and, where in my hunger I have not licked it, you can still see traces of red. You see . . . they don't keep the lions in cages anymore. They're in an open-plan area with a moat, and there wasn't any way to get to them. I stared at them for a while, watched a lioness relentlessly pacing, another caged creature shut off like myself – but that would not meet my eyes.

I moved on.

There's a lot of rubbish in the zoo: monkeys playing with their privates, stuck-up giraffes, and stuff so dozy it wouldn't take any notice of you if you fucked it. I wandered through it all – searching, searching, and came at last to the polar bears. God what animals! I've heard they're the most dangerous, unpredictable beasts in the world. The king killers. They certainly looked it in their elevated rocky area just a few yards away across a low rail and moat.

I stood and observed them, their tiny eyes gleaming evil, the dribble dripping from their long yellow fangs. And it seemed to me, if they tried, they could easily leap the moat and rail between us; and, running amok on this side of it, their massive claws gash through the bellies of every human being here.

Perhaps that still included me . . .

'Come on then!' I leaned over the rail and screamed at them. '*Come on!*'

And one of them came.

It loped from the rocks, padded, huge-pawed down to the edge of its parapet and stood there on the very brink, its long neck swaying out towards me, tiny eyes peering savagely from its pointed head. It opened its mouth. Only yards from me, I saw the huge yellow fangs, smelt the rotting flesh reek of its breath. It gave a whimpering grunt; its muscles seemed to tense beneath its thick fur – and in sudden real fear I backed, backed till I felt another rail behind me.

For a moment I was frozen. Then I could move and did. I did not wait to continue this silly test. I left that place and the zoo and had walked half the way back across Regent's Park, before the hackles down my back finally died.

I felt tired and futile. Other than scaring myself, I had

achieved nothing. Seeing a park bench beneath a tree to my left, I went to it and sat there.

It was late afternoon now, the shadows long along the grass. I remembered I had sat on a park bench before; there had been an ancient mad whore. When had that been? I could not be sure. The past was a jumble. The future . . .

I didn't have much time.

I was suddenly convinced *they* were close, and uneasily scanned the green space around me; but saw only walkers, parents perambulating children in the distance . . .

And, much closer, a squirrel.

It was only yards away and proceeding, feathery tail extended, in a series of charming hops towards my bench. There are lots of squirrels in Regent's Park and they are very tame. Keeping otherwise still, I slowly held out my hand to it, half open along the top of the bench, the way a man might offering food. If you're quiet and gentle, these squirrels are so tame they'll come right up and eat out of your hand. And clearly this one must have seen me. It hopped to the bench, paused, sitting alertly on its hind legs on the grass less than a yard from my feet. I stayed very still, my hand extended in offering. It was so close I could see its nose twitch, the fine whiskers on its grey face.

It hopped to the arm of the bench; hardly pausing, moved from there up to the bench's back, along which my beckoning hand lay. Nose working, it advanced right up to my hand.

I grabbed it.

You have to be quick to do that. I was. Like a snake. My fingers fastened around it. I held it tight in my hand, could feel its little legs kicking as it tried to squirm free. I think it was trying to bite me too, and to hold it more securely, I tightened my thumb and forefinger around its throat.

I found my hand continued to tighten.

It had to. I could not let this little life go now, escape me. I held the tiny furred creature in my fist and, as I continued to squeeze, could feel its heart battering like a frantic trapped bug against my palm. It gave a hissing squeak. I squeezed tighter. Its little red eyes began to bulge, its tongue come through its long front teeth from its throat. The eyes bulged more; the tongue continued to lengthen; blood burst from the nose.

And then it wasn't moving anymore.

Slowly, I uncurled my palm. It was wet. The thing had excreted, dying, and lay there now, its body no longer than my hand. I had to do it, don't you see. And what is a squirrel? Only a form of rat that lives in trees.

On reflection, it seems absurd that my eyes were brimming through my smile, as I tilted my hand and let the little carcass fall.

# CHAPTER EIGHTEEN

Life gives life. Even the life of a rodent, and taking it had given me substance. I knew that for certain, as I strode south across Regent's Park in the twilight. I could feel the strength, the power, surging through me – much as I had when I'd pushed that whining brat down the escalator, and caused his blood to flow.

But, just as then, the sensation did not last. A little blood, the life of a squirrel, is not enough . . .

It was getting dark now. Quite rapidly. And as I walked I began to notice the rustle of dead leaves moving across the grass – and all at once the thin dead branches of the trees around me turned to nets in the gathering dusk.

I started to walk a little faster; and it was then I became certain I was being followed – and knew by what.

How do you know something like that? I knew it from the prickling of the skin on my face and hands, from the coldness on my spine, from the way the hair at the back of my neck was starting to rise. I lengthened my stride. Hurried on. They . . . *they* . . . were still there. But how close? I knew I should not look back, but could not stand not knowing . . .

Abruptly, I stopped and turned to look behind me. The visibility was down; I could not see very far and perhaps – perhaps – that movement that flickered behind the trees at the very borderline of my vision was only shadow.

I did not believe that it was, was almost certain these were grotesquely humped shapes, massing in the near darkness and, not quite able to see them, was still in no doubt what they were. And then, like spectral figures, wisps of fog, I imagined that they began to drift towards me, across – but not touching – the grass.

I turned and I fled. Out of the park. Out to the street, lit and hustling and holding back the desolation of the shades of night. They would not follow me through this hurrying place of hard matter. They did not belong here.

Did I?

I settled to a walk, shook off speculation. And memory. After all, I had a plan. And I was learning . . .

I walked. Clip-clip. Feet solid on a pavement. Solid on some pavement somewhere. I walked a long way. Right down to Oxford Street and then along it, trying not to look into all its soulless windows at my ghostly reflection as it passed. There was nothing behind me now. For a time I had shaken them. All the way down New Bond Street I went, all the way to Piccadilly, thinking, thinking all the time. I had no use or need for the people or things that I passed there.

But, turning into Piccadilly, I needed confirmation again.

My legs were tired, my feet sore, and perhaps because I had not eaten since – I could not remember but, Jesus, I am hungry now – my head was strangely light. Whatever, I'd had enough wandering. While there was still time, I must act.

People now. Opposite Green Park tube station, there was a newspaper vendor. I went to his stand and helped myself to a paper, and made no attempt to pay him. But he did not appear to care, peering preoccupied at something across the street, and it was impossible to tell whether he could have noticed me if he tried. At least I had the newspaper, though. All right, it was far more cumbersome than any *Evening Standard* had the right to be, but I held it. Had lifted it from the stand. No . . . non-thing . . . could do that.

I walked a little way further, carrying the paper, firmly displacing it in time and space. Then I stopped and laboriously tore it – I could do that – tore it into pieces, scattered them among the rush-hour people to the pavement. I might be fading, yes, but I was still able to influence matter. That newspaper knew. It knew me – just as the squirrel had. I existed in more than my mind.

I stepped off the pavement into the road.

There was a squeal of tyres. Looking to my right, I saw cars braking sharply just by me. Hah, I thought, that proves it also! The conspiracy might be universal, but it didn't stretch to the point of running me down. I felt good about that as I crossed. Until I looked left – and saw I'd crossed at a lights – and that they were red.

I stood on the opposite pavement. It was swarming with people, hurrying, jostling, ant-hiving by to a tube entrance just to my right, and I realised it was only people – helpless sheep-herded people – that gave you any reality in this world.

Then, as that knowledge came floating to me, I saw the arches and the bulk of the Ritz Hotel. I started towards it. There was a wind at my back. I had never been in the place before – why should I? – but I went in then.

Ever been to the Ritz? It's ritzy. A place of light and elegance: a large lobby, the back of it raised to a rostrum and, as I entered, people at tables there, taking tea. Tea – my god, how civilised! And above them all a light high ceiling with mouldings of gold. It was the sort of place that makes you feel good even as it impresses you and, after the grubby street, a vision of another life style and age. I would sit at one of those tables, take tea there. Perhaps engage in elegant conversation with a lady at an adjacent table. I drew myself up, studiedly walked towards that wide raised area. Naturally no-one looked at me – but how ill-mannered it would have been, if they had!

When I climbed the steps that led to the dias, however, I saw every table there was taken.

That was not good and I almost turned away, but then thought: no, I will not be cheated of this – of my tea – and I looked around for a table with a free place at it and, seeing one, went to it.

A bald head fringed with blond hair that flaked dandruff onto a Saville Row collar was nodding at a spiky permed blonde, 'Would you mind if I sat here?' I asked it.

The head went on nodding, the voice it emitted a drone. 'Is this seat taken?'

The head gave a jerk that might have been assent or part of the conversation; but it didn't turn and I did not care. The chair was already the right distance out from the table, and I placed myself at it, midway between the man and the woman. She looked briefly in my direction, looked back at the man. He had not altered his flow. He was explaining about his wife. I smiled at them paternally, listened for a moment to his intense low monotone, but found it as uninteresting as the blonde obviously did and, leaning back in my chair, looked around for some service. There was one languid waiter visible, but his attention was occupied, so I turned back to our table. The man was leaning so far across it now, he was near to spraying his dandruff in the girl's eyes. From a face as perfectly set as concrete, they assessed him steadily. I looked round for another waiter, saw one facing my way and gestured to him. He seemed to react and start towards me, but just as I was triumphantly thinking what I'd order, veered aside and went on to another table. At which time, I heard a note of pleading and, looking back at my table once more, saw the girl shake her head abruptly and get up. Looking stunned, the man rose an instant later and hurried after her. I watched them go. That girl was a long way from being any girl.

And so . . . I sat at their table, the debris of their tea on the sullied white table cloth – a little battlefield, where the man had lost – a big silver teapot, used cups, a plate of untouched cakes. Why not, I thought. I looked round once more for service and not getting it, turned back and reached for the teapot.

I could not lift it.

Not even an inch. It sounds absurd, but it was grotesque. I couldn't believe if for a second. Then I tried again. This time, using two hands, I was able to reach across the table and lug it to me – just. I got it in front of me and my muscles were as strained as if I'd lifted two hundred kilos. Jesus, what had they put in that pot? I took off the lid . . .

Nothing.

The teapot was empty. Yes. I stared at it and everything churned and scrambled inside me – and then came out.

'*Why?*' I screamed at the room, 'Why are you doing this to me?'

I struggled from my chair, stood there slavering round me, but from all that august assemblage I had not even produced the reaction of a gentle yawn.

'*What have I ever done to you?*' I shrieked, and beat my fist down on the table and, I believe, stamped my foot.

Whatever . . . no-one took any notice and, insane with rage and frustration, I turned on the table, tried to lift and overturn it; but the task was too much for my limited powers, and the thing barely swayed.

I stumbled away. I could not accept it, any of it, the lack of reaction alone . . . it had to be deliberate. These mincing mannequins, parading through their empty motions, while all this was happening – to *me*. I glared around at them, wheeled to the rostrum's steps . . .

And it was there that I knew how to get them, how to force them, to see.

Slowly, on the very top step, I turned. Looking over the room I told it quite reasonably, 'All right you dirty indifferent bastards, see what you think of this!'

And I reached down and unzipped myself and yanked it out.

I waited then: for sudden intake of breath, averted faces of women, outrage of men; for hurrying footsteps behind me. But, Hitch . . . oh Jesus, there was nothing. There I was – me – respectable, a teacher – exposing myself in front of perhaps all of fifty people in the lobby of the Ritz – and no-one, not one of them, took any notice at all.

I could not stand that. The slightest reaction and, god knows, middle-class and conditioned as I am, I might well have peed with delight all over their fine carpet; but this – this . . . I zipped myself up, wheeled, and near to blubbering, ran out of that place.

A doorway.

Somewhere down Piccadilly. With everything surging, pounding, breaking, a surf of glass crashing to fragments on the rocks inside me and the sounds of grunts and giggles washing in and out of my brain as relentless and manic as the sea.

I was crouching in a doorway, bent over like a fixing junky in the dark of the shadows of Piccadilly while the lights of life went by.

I felt my back click straight.

Like an unclasped flick-knife, I jerked up. I came out of

that doorway, Hitch. I went on.

Things.

So many things to do. I went on up to Piccadilly Circus. Lights and louts. I was not broken. I went on right through.

I went down the steps of the Leicester Square lavatory.

Do you remember I told you about Roger Walsh, Claire's Foreign Office friend? Well he'd told me once that Special Branch or MI something-or-other had this particular pisser wired; that it was here, in fact, that a certain TV actor and MP had been observed and filmed in the act of unnatural union. Imagine that! You know, I stood there that night and looked round that dreary, ugly smelling urinal and I believed it. It seemed a perfectly fit sort of place from which to run our affairs.

'What have I done?' I asked it.

But all it gave me in the way of an answer was the hack of a man in a trenchcoat, propped up in a urinal, spitting at the end of a row.

'Why me?' I yelled again, 'Why *me*?'

Silence.

'I never did anyone any harm!'

And then, as my last words died, I realised that perhaps that was the trouble . . .

It had a fine echo that place. But the powers that rule our lives from lavatories are as blind and as deaf, and in the long run I suppose quite as unlikely, as those in the skies. They gave me nothing but my words.

The man in the trenchcoat shook himself, then swayed out of his urinal and came towards me and the exit, doing up his flies.

'I want to stick it up your arse,' I told him.

But he just belched and went by. He was only a drunk.

Then it came to me – what I'd done – and I whooped and nearly fell down with laughter. It was magnificent, eh? My language, that place! They filled me with a rapture of delight. Roaring and dancing I Gene Kellyed up the stairs of that bog and would have turned a cartwheel in the street above, if I'd known how – and in fact did do a little tap dance, and even a few bars of 'Singing in the Rain'. Ah-ha, the joy of life! I took a couple of pound notes from my pocket and flung them in the air – it seemed the thing to do – and my laughing went wilder, because I knew no-one would notice them. And they didn't, those hordes – just rushed by. I kicked at the money. Then bent down and picked it up. You see . . . I wasn't mad. No, I was free. I considered delivering my superbly subtle come-on again. To a cop, perhaps, this time; but you can never find a policeman when you need one – and a joke repeated is never so good – and – maybe – it had never been that funny . . .

I couldn't work my key in the lock when I got home and I rang the bell and heard it ring, but there wasn't any answer and, looking round, I could not see Claire's car. Glancing up, I noticed the drawing-room window was slightly open and just for a moment considered doing a Batman up the drain-pipe. But then I saw the waiting spikes of the railings below and was not ready for them. Claire could not be gone forever.

I must wait.

It was cold.

I could not remember what I'd come out with, but did not have a coat now. I found them . . . imprisoning, you see, so I started walking back and forth outside the door to keep warm, and considered doing a circuit of the square; but it occurred to me I might miss Claire and – if I did – might never get in.

And where would I go to then?

What?

I'm sorry, I thought for a moment you spoke then, that you said, 'Where you're going anyway – straight down the road to hell.'

It had a beauty out there that night.

Piles of leaves like lives in the street, all tumbled and discarded, and here and there tidied to be taken away; smoky breath in the light from our old-fashioned street lamps; and the occasional passer with head crunched into coat collar, hurrying home as if in a drinking chocolate commercial. It was seasonal – a true London Autumn night – and that has a scent. And a calm.

Then Claire's car came smoking down the approach

street, braked fiercely for a parking space outside our door, but overshot it; and finally backed in with a jerk that scrunched a rear tyre against the curb. Dear Claire, she always drove with such style!

She tumbled out of the Renault, arms chock-a-block with carrier bags, and I leaned against the railings, hands in pockets, and watched her trying to steady them under her chin as she locked the car door.

'My darling!' I said in a whisper.

Vision partly obscured by the packages she was juggling now in her arms, she went past me up the stairs, fumbling into her handbag for her door key, getting the wrong one first . . .

Where was I while all this went on? Why, right behind her? Breathing down her neck. I wondered if she found my breath hot – and admired the way she managed to ignore me. I mean, it didn't just take perserverence, it took courage. I might have lost my cool.

She got the hall door open – and dropped a package. She leaned against the door to stop it closing while she picked the package up, and I stepped in over her. I went to the top of the communal stairs then and looked down at her and waited. Clever Claire. Most people, being looked at, can sense it; but she was sorting through the mail on the hall table with all the unconcern of a woman alone.

Remarkable.

And then she managed to come up the stairs without once lifting her eyes from its treads.

I waited at the top of the stairs till, only inches from me, she came and put her key in our flat's door. Then as she swung it open, I preceeded her in, flitted into this love nest of ours ahead of her – not perhaps the most romantic of homecomings, but certainly one with a . . . difference, eh?

Sitting on the stairs outside the drawing-room, I watched and waited while Claire went into the kitchen, deposited one of her packages, then came on up towards me. I did not get out of her way. I was sitting across half a step and wanted to see how she'd negotiate me – and have to admit she did it adroitly: walking past me so damn naturally, appearing not to see me – but not stepping on me either.

Clever Claire.

I sat and watched her. She looked in through the drawing-room doorway, then – still carrying two bags – went on up the stairs. And started to whistle. Whistle. My god, in all the years I'd never heard her do that. It was a ghastly sound!

I rose and followed her up to the bedroom. She'd thrown her bags on the bed and, still making this throttled kettle noise, was unpacking them. She'd bought clothes and, shaking out a dress, held it before her in front of the mirror, frowning as she inspected it. She seemed to find the thing satisfactory, though, and tossed it on the bed and did more rummaging. I took a chair behind her; watched as she wriggled into a pair of jeans, then examined them – back, front, sideways – pivoting in front of the mirror. Interestingly, I could see myself reflected in the glass behind her, but she managed to ignore me, smoothing denim over hip, pulling it tighter into crotch . . . they were far too young for her those jeans.

I looked at myself in the mirror and shook my head. I grinned. It was a cunning grin and nice to see. But I wasn't going to do a Claire and go all drooly over myself and, waving a hand at my image in farewell, got up and went down to the kitchen.

I badly needed food.

But, finding a can of ravioli in the kitchen, managing to heave it down from the shelf, I was unable to open it. I tried. Not enough substance though. Not enough to force metal jaws to mash through metal; to turn that unturnable wheel.

I stood instead.

I heard the can-opener hit the floor, but my eyes were on the mirror over the breafast nook. It says something about Claire that she had a mirror in the kitchen. I thought of her. Upstairs, whistling after her shopping spree. She was cheerful as – as a woman let free. I looked at myself in the mirror. I was so calm. I opened the fridge. A two-year-old could open that fridge. I took out bread. As I put it down, I saw the 'Kitchen Devil' on a working surface – light and incredibly sharp. I picked it up, gazed into the gleam of its blade and raised it, watching myself in the mirror now.

What would Claire do if I sliced off my ear? Left it waiting for her on the stairs. It was an amusing thought, but I sliced the knife through the bread instead, and turned my mind to other things.

I was so calm it was sublime.

What do we really know about the nature of man's existence – and the drugs that can reduce it to the point where you fade away?

What do we know of the extent to which our substance is determined by the minds of others – and of how, when no-one, not a single person in the world, thinks of you, you wink out – and cease to be?

And what do we know of other dimensions – worlds that overlap within worlds?

I'll tell you, my fine oriental friend: we know fuck all.

I think it was the ravioli that finally did it.

Showed that there was no more time; that, if I did not somehow re-establish my essence right now, I would soon be unable to feed myself and – even if things that I would not think about did not happen first – I would then simply die of starvation.

So it all came down to one thing: I must make the ultimate act of reality, cement myself forever into this world. I knew the way now.

I would need a little help from Claire.

# CHAPTER NINETEEN

I am hungry, terribly hungry, and the ache of my long empty belly does not make it easy to think. Perhaps that is why, when I talk to you, my words sometimes run away with me and I come out more savage than the thing that I am.

I am really a very mild man.

I've got the bulk and weight to be something else, I suppose, but I'm not. A kid, some bottles, a squirrel – what are those? I'm gentle, Hitch. It's important you understand that. It'll help you appreciate the courageousness of the thing that I did.

Because, you see, I had no way else to go. No other course. I had to do it. It was the only way I could make myself . . . real. Extreme, you say? Perhaps. But then, consider my position; put yourself in my shoes.

You see?

The night I finally decided, I'd eaten my bread and slept; and I think that was the first full night of sleep I can remember for – for I don't know how long. And then – whatever day that was – I woke and knew what I must do. It was already almost too late. I had slipped some more in the night, lost more hold, and the very act of dressing that day was too much for me, and I could only manage socks and a dressing-gown – and even the feel of its cotton was as iron on my body and its weight like a cloak of chains. Yet that was nothing. Because, when I went to the kitchen, I found I could not now open the fridge.

Knowing what had to be done, though, I kept my head and did not panic.

I went round the kitchen, managing what I could. Most of our wall units were touch-catched and opened when I hit them, but the drawers were beyond me. It didn't matter.

What I needed was on a working surface and I was able to eat some Jaffa Cakes from a top cupboard and then carried the pack along with the other thing to the drawing-room.

I put them on the table – just there – then went back to the kitchen and fetched everything else I could manage that was faintly edible – bits of fruit, crisps, a pack of Rowntrees jelly, some popadums, raw pasta, rice, cereal – I brought them all into the drawing-room and made a horde of them here.

It was as well to be careful, you see. I didn't think I would need these supplies; but, supposing my plans misfired ... and the kitchen door were to slam shut, how would I ever get at the food again?

Water was less easy. Two-handedly wrestling with the kitchen tap grooved my hands, but did not move the metal and I could not now wield a shoe sufficiently hard to knock the taps on as I had once before. I wasn't beaten, though. Indeed, I was getting more cunning and resourceful all the time. I took a tea towel; managed to a stab a hole in it and get that over the spokes of the tap. Then I picked up the other end of the towel and, using all the weight and strength I had, heaved. I think I must have been employing some sort of leverage principle. Whatever ... the thing came on. Triumphant, I had a good long drink. Then I left the tap running and, before going back to the drawing-room, kicked the towel as best I could against the door to wedge it, so it could not slam shut against me. I was taking every precaution – and probably unnecessarily.

After all, I had only the day to wait out before Claire came home and saved me.

Dear Claire.

I turned on the television and sat on the sofa here, eating Jaffa Cakes and watching programmes for schools and it was really rather relaxing. Now and then I'd get up and go to the windows and look out into the gardens. It was sunny. The trees were almost bare. At morning break, children came out and ran round screaming. The only thing I didn't like about standing there looking out of that window was – sometimes I saw movement in the room behind me, well not really saw it, more sensed it at the corners of my eyes. Not pictures or chairs or anything. Not like that other time. No.

This was more a . . . presence . . . that had not been in the room before. But when I turned my head to look, there was nothing. It was unsettling, though. Just a little. You know what I fancied? That it – whatever it was – was playing a game with me, a sort of 'Grandmother's Footsteps' – creeping up on me to the borders of my vision – defying me to see it!

But that was only a little thing. It did not break the serenity of that day. Oh yes, that's how you feel. That's what a man finally feels like when his life has come to one single purpose – one thing he has to do.

I waited.

I let the sound of the television blur to a meaningless drone in my mind and then, listening within myself a while, could hear other sounds: the pound of the blood surfing round in my brain; a faint caw of gulls on the wing above that tide, calling to me from far reaches . . .

I waited.

In the afternoon I think I slept, the sun slanting over the treetops in cold slivers of ice into the room and making patterns against my closed eyes. Dancing little maggots running up and down a curving screen. In red.

Red like my body and the carpet there.

I woke. The fire-ice had gone from the room and the sun was below the houses across the square and the shades were coming. The light in the room was on, though. Till the bulb burned out, there was no way now it could not be.

I wondered what Claire would think about that. Bless her heart, I think I may have said some things against her, but how wrong can you be? God knows, life with me could not have been easy. But she always stuck loyally by.

And I'm sure will stick by me forever.

I went for a little walk. Round the room. It's a nice room, isn't it? My reclining body, all day on the sofa, had made almost no impression on those soft cushions, you know. I came and sat down on them again. Right here, and finished off the Jaffa Cakes and sang little songs in my mind. The dressing-gown was now far too uncomfortable, so I took it off and sat here in just my socks. That was much better. I wasn't cold.

Slowly, whatever makes the night and day go, made it begin to grow darker. As it did, I noticed myself begin to materialise like an apparition reflected in the window behind the television – an interesting sight, a pale naked figure against the gathering black – and yet serene, for somewhere along the way, my face had set with the permanence of rigor mortis into a smile.

And so the evening came: my reflection growing firmer, programmes moving inexorably across the screen beneath it, cartoons giving way to old children's programmes and finally to grown-up news. I can analyse that, the changes. But they all seemed exactly the same. Patterns and sounds without significance swimming like torpid fish through my brain.

It was somewhere in the middle of some quiz show that I heard her key in the lock.

'Stephen?'

I jolted. I was up. I grabbed what I needed. Did I imagine that – that she called my name? Her? Why had she come home like that, this time? It didn't matter. I was standing now, ready, and she did not call again and I could picture her as I heard the faint sounds: taking off her rather tired coat, hanging it on the peg outside the kitchen; and then her feet on the stairs, and they sounded tired too. For a moment I thought – suppose she goes on up to the bathroom? But she didn't. She came in.

I was waiting.

'Stephen?' she said, as she walked in.

For the barest instant, I looked at her. She looked frail, worn – but why should that delay me? I didn't hesitate. Not long. I held the 'Kitchen Devil' in both my hands. I stepped in front of her. With all my strength I swung that knife at her throat.

Ah!

I was weak, oh yes, next to nothing. But the blade of that knife was tungsten tipped surgical steel. Did I ever tell you what the advertisement for it said? 'A new Kitchen Devil won't make every piece of scrag end you buy taste like prime tender fillet – only *slice* like it!' Claire's throat was much softer than scrag end. It parted like a great wide opening mouth and everything gushed out.

I do not think I'll describe the next bit.

It was not quick and I did not know there was so much blood in a body. See for yourself. See it all over my nakedness, the carpet and the furniture here. As I say, she did not die at once, but gave a strangely machine-sounding 'woo' – very like a vacuum cleaner disconnected – and her hands clutched to her throat. They tried to hold it together, but couldn't and the blood pumped through from her fingers. Her legs wobbled. She crashed back against the door, slamming it closed behind her. Then her kness went and, tottering forward, she fell across the armchair.

She tossed and she pumped there.

And there she finally died.

I stood and looked down at her. I had cut well: the head was almost half off, the face amazingly pale with no blood left in the body. I was sticky from it and shaking, but looking down at her then, I felt good. I had done it! Something more . . . influential than anything I'd ever done in my life! My doubts were gone. I was certain, had proof incontestable. And briefly, but beyond any question, Claire and the world knew it too.

Knew that I was real.

# CHAPTER TWENTY

That should, of course, have been the happy ending.

I felt so powerful. There would be nothing now that could resist me. But, when I put my gore-red hand on it, I could not turn the doorknob.

How long ago was that?

God knows – time is a thing from some other place – but it seems almost forever: the light always on, the television, and Claire there – slowly changing, ripening, her black-coated mouth now gaping full and voluptuous to the flies that walk in and out of it.

It's been nice having this little chat. I've all sorts of theories about how it all came to be, and would like to ask my wife about them; but the only sounds that will ever come from her now are the bubbling gasses of her decomposition, and the hiss of the maggots in her flesh.

One thing is certain, I am not the only one.

Every year, hundreds of people simply . . . disappear. I remember the voice on the telephone, the man I saw wordlessly mouthing in Hyde Park. And, of course, the . . . unfinished . . . creatures that came to me first in a dream, then in the London that could not be. It is clear to me why I saw them more and more, where that dusty room leads, where I am going . . .

And what I am become.

Ah, but admit it, I had a good go, did not let myself be taken easy! Not that any of it was much use – sorry about that, Claire – but what is a man if he doesn't try? Then – then he is truly nothing.

Of course, just here in this place, I am little better than that – trapped here, with you, my excrement, those packs of empty food and Claire. The gods have a mocking humour. There was nothing in life Claire loathed so much as television – now she's watching it into eternity. Ironic, isn't it? Mind you, though her eyes are open, they are not very seeing eyes. More hazed blobs of jelly pointing dully towards the screen . . .

Sometimes, just sometimes, it worries me when I look at her there that she is going to turn her head and point them at me, those dull eyes. In my weakness once I even tried to prop a cushion up to hide them, but the thing fell off her and I cannot lift it now.

No matter.

Has any of what I told you registered? I had to do it, don't you see? And though I did not manage to reverse the process, I proved my reality. When you think about it, what can matter more than that?

Reality where? Ah . . . well . . . increasingly not here, but no doubt where I am going, and I'm sure there are points of contact and perhaps – perhaps – when I have got there you will hear the click of my laughter some night in the wind. Ah! And it will matter as much as all that we do and are done to by each other.

Visions.

Seeing clearer now. There are things falling down in my mind. Old buildings. I can see light through their rubble. It is grey.

The smell of all that ripe meat is making me salivate and I cannot stand it.

I go to the window. I look out into the rain. I think I see them there, my people: eyeless and leper faced – gathering.

Ah, Hitch!

I'm not sure I've always been very polite to you through this, old son. You must forgive me. It hasn't always been easy. Though telling you was comfort. You know, if – if you could only walk and I could open that door and the one below, we could go out together you and I, take a stroll round the gardens. I'd like that. If *they* were not there.

There are one or two more every hour. When they are enough – quite soon – they will come.

Look, Hitch – a sparrow! Huddling there on the window sill, trying to get in out of the rain. In here! Poor little bird, mad sod. I wish I could let it in and feed it, but of course I can do nothing and – what would I feed it on?

Listen!

Was that the door, the downstairs door? Did you hear? That swinging, that creak – it's open. Ah! Now it closes. There is something on the stairs, climbing the stairs, more than one, a soft squeaking as of a grey blind rat pack, faceless things . . . the sound is rising. Nearer. The creatures of my kingdom are come.

The gibbering horde.

They are nearly up my stairs. Behind that closed door at the end of the room they are gathering. I hear their squeaking, their sewn-mouthed mewing outside on the landing. Behind just that door. Very soon, the doorknob will turn . . .

And this time there will be no escaping them.

I would like to say goodbye now – properly – to shake you by the hand. But, being a tape recorder, you of course do not have a hand. Still – it has done me good to talk to you and perhaps, if anyone ever hears this, if it happens to them, they will know what to do: Kill. Kill everything while they can.

I left it too late.

I have almost no substance now. Am that skeleton man I once saw in the mirror of the bath, a shadow that faceless hordes will take to the endless dusty wasteland of shadows.

But, ah Claire, before they do . . . I will make the final act of union with you – man and wife become one.

I will feed.

Something has gone terribly wrong in the charnel house of science . . . something that must never see the light of day.

# CHIMERA

## Stephen Gallagher

Any government cover-up is news but this time journalist Peter Carson knows he's onto something big. A top research laboratory on the remote Cumbrian moors is cut off from all outside contact. Rumours of an accident at the pioneering Jenner Clinic spread beyond the armed roadblocks and seep through the massive official news blackout.

Dr Jenner's work matters to the government. It matters enough to have a blank cheque, high security cover and the best technicians in the country. But something has gone badly wrong. The project that has no room for mistakes has produced a result so terrible that it must never see the light of day. And now the evidence must be destroyed whatever the cost . . .

**ADVENTURE/THRILLER**     0 7221 3757 5     £1.75

# THE THIRST THAT NEVER DIES . . .

## THEY THIRST

## ROBERT R. McCAMMON

The shots whistled high over the boy, striking the man in the face and throat. Papa screamed – a resounding scream of rage – as he was flung backward to the floor where he lay with his face in shadow and his boots in red embers.

And then a slow, scraping noise came from the other side of the room.

The boy spun round to look.

Papa was rising to his feet. Half of his face was gone, leaving his chin and jaw and nose hanging by white, bloodless strings. The remaining teeth glittered with light, and the single pulped eye hung on one thick vein across the ruined cavern where the cheekbone had been. White nerves and torn muscles twitched in the hole of the throat. The man staggered up, crouched with his huge hands twisted into claws. When he tried to grin, only one side of the mouth remained to curve grotesquely upward.

And in that instant both boy and woman saw that he did not bleed . . .

**HORROR**          0 7221 5876 9          £1.75

# GRAHAM MASTERTON

## THE MASTER OF HORROR

It's late at night . . . the wind is howling around the door . . . the fire flickers eerily in the grate . . . and you're alone . . .

Now's the time to pick up one of Graham Masterton's spine-tingling horror novels, novels like CHARNEL HOUSE, the scarifying story of a house that's anything but normal, or REVENGE OF THE MANITOU, a tale of revenge more horrifying than you could ever imagine.

Read a Graham Masterton horror story tonight, but beware . . .

Enter the world of Graham Masterton at your own risk – you may never want to be alone again!

By Graham Masterton in Sphere Books:

A selection of bestsellers from SPHERE

**FICTION**

| | | |
|---|---|---|
| REMEMBRANCE | Danielle Steel | £1.95 ☐ |
| BY THE GREEN OF THE SPRING | John Masters | £2.50 ☐ |
| MISSION | Patrick Tilley | £1.95 ☐ |
| DECEPTIONS | Judith Michael | £3.95 ☐ |
| THREE WOMEN | Nancy Thayer | £1.75 ☐ |

**FILM & TV TIE-INS**

| | | |
|---|---|---|
| E.T. THE EXTRA-TERRESTRIAL | William Kotzwinkle | £1.50 ☐ |
| FAME | Leonore Fleischer | £1.50 ☐ |
| CONAN THE BARBARIAN | L. Sprague de Camp & Lin Carter | £1.25 ☐ |
| THE SWORD AND THE SORCERER | Norman Winski | £1.50 ☐ |
| GREASE 2 | William Rotsler | £1.25 ☐ |

**NON-FICTION**

| | | |
|---|---|---|
| ONE CHILD | Torey L. Hayden | £1.75 ☐ |
| DAM-BURST OF DREAMS | Christopher Nolan | £1.75 ☐ |
| THE COUNTRYSIDE COOKBOOK | Gail Duff | £5.95 ☐ |
| GREAT RAILWAY JOURNEYS OF THE WORLD | | £5.95 ☐ |

All Sphere books are available at your local bookshop or newsagent, or can be ordered direct from the publisher. Just tick the titles you want and fill in the form below.

Name _____

Address _____

_____

Write to Sphere Books, Cash Sales Department, P.O. Box 11 Falmouth, Cornwall TR10 9EN
Please enclose a cheque or postal order to the value of the cover price plus:
UK: 45p for the first book, 20p for the second book and 14p per copy for each additional book ordered to a maximum charge of £1.63.
OVERSEAS: 75p for the first book and 21p for each additional book.
BFPO & EIRE: 45p for the first book, 20p for the second book plus 14p per copy for the next 7 books, thereafter 8p per book.

*Sphere Books reserve the right to show new retail prices on covers which may differ from those previously advertised in the text or elsewhere, and to increase postal rates in accordance with the PO.*